"You excite me more each time I see you," Dev said, his arms around her.

Felicity pressed a hand to his jaw, and a lightning bolt seemed to shoot through her. "You generate some heat yourself."

"Do I?"

Though there was space between them, she felt their bodies must be fused, their hearts and lungs functioning as one.

"In all things that matter, Felicity Dobbs Abrams, I'm yours," Dev said.

"Those were the vows we wrote for our wedding," she answered, her voice shaking.

"Yes." He caught on his finger the tear that slipped down her cheek. "Don't cry, love."

"Is it too far gone, Dev? Can it come back?"

"It was never lost, Felicity," he said fiercely, and pressed his lips to hers. . . .

WHAT ARE *LOVESWEPT* ROMANCES?

They are stories of true romance and touching emotion. We believe those two very important ingredients are constants in our highly sensual and very believable stories in the *LOVESWEPT* line. Our goal is to give you, the reader, stories of consistently high quality that may sometimes make you laugh, sometimes make you cry, but are always fresh and creative and contain many delightful surprises within their pages.

Most romance fans read an enormous number of books. Those they truly love, they keep. Others may be traded with friends and soon forgotten. We hope that each *LOVESWEPT* romance will be a treasure—a "keeper." We will always try to publish

LOVE STORIES YOU'LL NEVER FORGET
BY AUTHORS YOU'LL ALWAYS REMEMBER

The Editors

LOVESWEPT® • 310

Helen Mittermeyer
Blue Flame

 BANTAM BOOKS
TORONTO • NEW YORK • LONDON • SYDNEY • AUCKLAND

BLUE FLAME

A Bantam Book / February 1989

If you would be interested in receiving protective vinyl
covers for your Loveswept books, please write to this address
for information:

Loveswept
Bantam Books
P.O. Box 985
Hicksville, NY 11802

ISBN 0-553-21961-8

Published simultaneously in the United States and Canada

PRINTED IN THE UNITED STATES OF AMERICA

O   0 9 8 7 6 5 4 3 2 1

One

Why did he have the prickly sensation that trouble was brewing, Dev Abrams wondered. Cold perspiration touched his skin. This wasn't Vietnam. There was no need to be on the alert.

Relax! he told himself. He was Dev Abrams, theater critic. He was at the lobby bar in the Schubert Theater in Manhattan, waiting for intermission to end. He breathed slowly, trying to force the tension from his body.

Damn! He knew what was causing his uneasiness. He'd thought he'd seen Felicity at Shea Stadium that afternoon. Not that it was unusual to imagine he'd seen her. His wife had been dead for years, but still . . .

He grabbed the drink the bartender had mixed for him and swallowed half of it in one gulp.

Dev didn't usually review plays on the weekend. Like many New Yorkers he left Manhattan on the weekends to stay at his country place in the Cats-kills. But this Saturday he'd remained in town to take his three godchildren to a Mets game. It was convenient, then, to review this play tonight, rather than during the week.

He barely listened to the chatter of his two lovely companions, Lena and Melba. Though they were delightful diversions and very good com-pany, he was running his critique of the first half of the play through his mind . . . and try-ing to bury the image of the raven-haired woman who had lived in him since the day he'd met her. Even though she was lost to him, Felicity was still woven into his being.

"But, Lena,"—Melba's excited voice penetrated his thoughts—"she has Cartier's window around her neck."

Dev languidly turned his head to see who his companions were talking about.

Shock punched every bit of oxygen out of his body. It couldn't be! His imagination had blown his mind away. His hand shook. When he tight-ened it on his glass, a few drops of whiskey spilled on his hand. Felicity! She was standing there! But it couldn't be. He'd identified her and Es-ther's bodies, their jewelry. His glass dropped from his hand to the carpeted floor.

"Dev!" Lena exclaimed. "You splashed me. I'm glad the glass didn't break. Dev? What's the mat-ter with him, Melba?"

"I don't know. Dev?"

Dev didn't hear the question. *Was* it his imagination? She was more slender than he remembered, her lissome body giving no clue that it had once carried a child. Her tall, sleek form was garbed in a shimmering black silk dress that swathed her like a second skin, revealing every curve and plane of her body until it ended in a kick ruffle around her ankles. Her alabaster skin was enhanced by the ebony material, and her violet eyes were as bright as amethyst. Queenly and elegant, she drew assessing glances from both sexes.

Lena touched his arm. "Are you sick, Dev?"

"No." He forced the word out between tight lips.

A roaring had filled his head, obliterating Lena, Melba, everyone in the lobby except her. Felicity was alive! How could that be? Why was she here? Why hadn't she contacted him? That wasn't her twin; that was Felicity. Who were the two men standing beside her? And what about those three other men hovering behind her—swarthy, brawny men in dark suits.

As though his body were weighed down by iron clamps, he moved toward her clumsily, quite sure he wouldn't turn a hair if she went up in smoke. Was he actually in his own house dreaming this? How many times had he pictured her walking, strolling, running back into his life!

He was no more than three feet from her when he noticed the dark-suited men closing ranks around her. He didn't stop. Felicity seemed not to notice, not pausing in her conversation with the other two men.

One of the dark suits moved in front of him. "Pardon me, sir."

"Get out of my way," Dev said, unconsciously clenching his fists.

At the sound of his voice Felicity turned. Blood drained from her face, leaving it stark white against the black of her gown. "Dev? Dev, it can't be you."

Her voice was thin in disbelief, her body swaying like a leaf in the wind. They stared at each other for a long moment, both stunned, then Felicity's eyes fluttered and she fainted.

"Damn! Felicity!" Dev shoved aside the man blocking him and dove toward her. He caught her and they fell to the floor together, his body cradling hers.

He knew instantly that she was pounds lighter, her beautiful breasts slightly less full, but her skin was still smooth and soft.

People crowded around them, their voices rising and falling in confusion. Dev barely noticed. All of his attention was focused on Felicity.

"Dev," she whispered, not opening her eyes.

"I'm here. I'm here, Felicity."

"You're dead." She opened her eyes.

He shook his head, a wry smile twisting his mouth. "A slight exaggeration, darling. I'm here with you. But I thought *you* were dead." He frowned at her. "You fainted. I'm taking you to the hospital."

"You will unhand Madame dai Haaji," a man's voice above them said. "Or you will die."

Dev looked up into the hard black eyes of one of the men who had been standing beside Felicity.

"I'm all right, Abdul," Felicity said.

She pulled herself free of Dev's arms and stood up. Dev stood as well, never looking away from the tall, dark-haired man. Instinct told him the man's threat to kill him had not been idle.

"I am Abdul ben Hashallah of the Dahrainian consulate," the man said. "It is my job to protect Madame dai Haaji."

"Not any longer, Abdul," Felicity said in a low voice. "I'm back in my own country now."

"Madame, you will always have the interest of the Dahrainian people," Abdul ben Hashallah told her stiffly.

"There's no need," she said.

"Excuse me, sir." The second man, an American, moved closer to Dev, but stopped at Abdul's side. "I'm Jarred Hamilton, Madame dai Haaji's lawyer. If you could tell me who you—"

"After we take her to a doctor," Dev said, "I'll answer any and all questions." He lifted her in his arms, glaring at the men surrounding him. He surmised the three dark-suited men were bodyguards. "You're welcome to accompany me, but for now, get out of the way."

"Dev, please. I'm all right."

Someone touched his arm and he turned blindly. "Yes?"

"Sir," the usher beside him said, "your two friends have returned to their seats."

"Tell them I won't be joining them, and that

they should go to supper without me and charge it to my account." He tightened his arms around Felicity when she stirred, trying to get free. "No. Stay still. I'm taking you to the hospital." He glanced at Abdul. "Tell one of your men to get a cab."

"I have already sent for our car," Abdul said.

"Good." Dev was aware of their disapproval of him and his taking charge of Felicity, but he ignored it. Maybe they were going along with him because they sensed he would tear down the building if they tried to separate him from her.

A stretch limousine was waiting out front. He settled Felicity in it, then sat beside her. Abdul and Jarred Hamilton sat facing them, while one of the bodyguards climbed in front beside the driver. Dev spoke Farsi, the Persian language, but Abdul was using a dialect Dev didn't understand as he swiftly gave instructions to the other two guards. The limousine pulled away from the curb, and Dev assumed the other men had been told to follow. He didn't care what any of them did, though, so long as no one tried to take Felicity from him again.

Felicity stared at Dev, wonder and confusion swirling in her mind. How could this be Dev, her husband who had died, and yet it was he. His face was the same, though his chiseled features looked sharper. His blue eyes were still like gleaming sapphires, yet she saw a glint of ice in them too. He'd always been tough, but now she sensed a granitelike hardness to him. He'd gone from tall, dark, and handsome to tall, dark, and lethal. What had happened to him in the past five years? How could he be alive when she'd been told the Iranians had executed him?

"I can't believe you're here," she blurted out.

"I'm here," he said. He glanced at Abdul and Jarred. "And I'm staying. Now sit still. We'll be there in a few minutes."

There was a hospital near the theater district, and the limousine was soon pulling up to the front entrance. In the treatment room the doctor who examined Felicity pronounced her fit.

"A little rapid pulse is all. Have you had a shock, Mrs. dai Haaji?"

"Yes."

"And you're sure she's fine?" Dev asked.

"Yes, I am."

The doctor looked a little offended at Dev's persistence, but Dev didn't care. He brushed past him and took Felicity's hands, relieved she was all right.

"What happened to you?" he asked, his voice low and hoarse with emotion. "Where have you been?"

"So much happened, Dev. It was like a weird fantasy. After you were imprisoned in Iran, I went to the American Embassy in Beirut every day, hoping to hear that you were okay, had been released. Then one day they told me you'd been executed."

"There were times in the prison when I wished they would get it over with, but it was another newsman they killed. They accused him of espionage. I didn't know until I'd been released that the Iranians had sent a photograph of the other man to the American government, and it had been misidentified. They thought it was me.

"By the time I got back to Beirut, you and Esther had been missing for a month. Later I was shown the burned bodies of a woman and a baby girl. I identified your wedding ring and the gold chain and cross we gave Esther when she was born."

Dev couldn't go on. He was caught in the wonder of her violet eyes. There were so many questions to ask, but all that was important was that she was there in front of him. He could reach out and touch her . . . kiss her. His arms slipped around her and he pressed his mouth to hers, feeling the lightning thrust of excitement that had always been part of touching Felicity.

Through the haze that engulfed her, Felicity realized Jarred and Abdul were staring at them. She tried to pull back, but her limbs were like overcooked pasta. "Dev. Don't." She couldn't quiet the wild beating of her heart. Dev. He touched her and brought her to stinging, wondrous life. It was as though she'd been in limbo for years and needed him to carry her from the gray world.

Dev released her and studied her heart-shaped face. Her eyes seemed larger, the slight upturning in the corners emphasized by her loss of weight. Had she always had those wonderful cheekbones? The Oriental cast to her features was an absurd contrast to her coloring, but not to the blue-black hair she'd twisted into a French knot. "Tell me what happened to you."

"After I heard you were dead I . . . I didn't know what to do. The American Embassy was making arrangements to get Esther and me back to the States. About a week after you were supposedly killed, I was on my way to the embassy with Esther when some shelling started near our apartment. We took cover in an abandoned building. When it was over and we left, five Muslim militiamen in a truck stopped us and made us go with them. They took what little money and jewelry we had and kept us for three days. We were rescued by a man from Dahrain called Haaji dai Haaji." She hesitated. "I . . . wasn't well. Your death, fearing for my and Esther's lives, had literally made me ill. Haaji took care of us, took us back with him to Dahrain. He told me he'd informed the American Embassy that Esther and I were alive and well, but . . ." She shrugged. "Those were crazy times. The message must have gotten garbled or lost." She stared at him, still not quite believing he was there. "If I had known *you* were alive, nothing would have kept me from finding you."

His grip tightened painfully on her hands. "Felicity . . ."

"I think we should go now," Abdul said abruptly. He moved close to the hospital bed Felicity was sitting on.

"Yes," Jarred Hamilton said. "I'll take you to your apartment, madame."

"No," Dev said. "I'm taking her."

Felicity lifted a hand for silence when the three men began to argue. "It's all right, Abdul, Jarred. I do need to talk to Mr. Abrams."

"Oh, is that his name?" Jarred asked, raising his brows when Dev glared at him. "You haven't told us much."

Abdul nodded. "That is true."

"Sorry," Dev said. "I have other things on my mind. The name's Dev Abrams." He shook hands with both men. "You needn't worry about anything. I'll get her home."

"I will call you later, madame," Abdul said stiffly.

She nodded. "Fine. Thank you, both of you."

After Abdul and Jarred left, Dev asked Felicity for her address. While she readied herself to leave, he made a call from the pay phone in the hall.

"I'm not drunk, Pace," he assured his friend Pacer Dillon. "I mean it. She's here with me in the hospital. Yeah, I know it's weird. I don't know everything that happened yet, but I soon will."

Outside the hospital Dev hailed a cab and helped her inside. "Abdul ben Hashallah and Jarred Hamilton seemed reluctant to leave you," he said after giving her address to the driver.

"They worry about me, but they know, now that I'm back in this country to stay, I won't need guards."

"And you needed them in Dahrain?"

"Yes." She hesitated. "A great deal has happened, Dev. There's so much you don't know."

"I"m aware of that. How long have you been in New York?"

"Only since Wednesday." She smiled faintly. "I've been meaning to call your old friend Con Wendel, just to get back in touch. I'm glad I didn't. He probably would have thought I was some crank playing a very cruel joke."

"And Esther?"

"Wonderful! She's finding the United States a bit strange, but she's managing." Her smile broadened. "Our little girl is a true cosmopolite. She speaks Farsi and Dahrainian and is becoming fluent in English and French."

Dev's throat tightened. He hadn't seen her grow from baby to little girl. He hadn't heard her first word, or seen her take her first step. He turned to Felicity. Her face was only erratically lit by the passing streetlights, but he sensed she was trying to keep some distance between them. Still, there was one thing he had to know now.

"They called you Madame dai Haaji."

"Yes. That was my name in Dahrain. Tell me what you've been doing, Dev."

Her evasiveness angered him, and he forced himself to cool off. Where she had been, what she had done, wasn't important. Having her beside him in the dingy cab, the real thing, in the flesh, his wife, was more important than anything. "I'm a theater critic, not a correspondent. I've written a couple of novels that have sold well. I've had a

little success in business." He shrugged. "Some of
the properties I've purchased have sold at a good
profit. My 'dabbling,' as Con calls it, has paid off.
I like business more than I thought I would."

"That's a surprise. You were never keen on it
when—when we were together."

"Things change."

"And you've been writing. How wonderful. I
would like to read your books."

"I'll get copies for you."

Felicity searched his face in the gloom of the
cab, the lights of Manhattan casting geometric
patterns across his features. What was he thinking? She was hating this conversation, hated them
sounding like two old friends who hadn't seen
each other for years and were catching up on
their lives before again going their separate ways.
But now that the shock of seeing Dev alive was
starting to wear off, anxiety was filling her. What
would he do when he found out the truth? She
had to tell him, but not now, not yet.

"And you're into real estate," she went on, filling the uncomfortable silence. "I find that hard to
take in." Her laugh was brittle.

"Do you? Believe it or not, I'm learning. Pacer
and Con are so good at it, I was bound to pick up
a thing or two. They felt I needed other . . . diversions besides my writing." The truth was, if Con
and Pacer hadn't pressed him to do more, and
more, and more those first couple of years, he
would have gone mad. "If things continue the way

they have been, the three of us might form a business partnership."

"Is this the Dev I knew?"

"I suppose not. In some ways he died in Beirut."

"Didn't we all." She bit her lip, pressing her fingers to her temples. She'd gone to hell and back. "It's been quite a night."

"I want you and Esther to stay at my place. I have a brownstone I rattle around in and there's plenty of room."

"Dev, don't push. Please. I'm staying in an apartment in a building leased by the Dahrainian government. I'll be there until I can find my own place."

He inhaled sharply. "And you don't think you should be with me?"

"Dev, I—"

"Why do they call you Madame dai Haaji?" The question was like a missile, zinging around the confines of the car, lethal and ready to explode.

The cab pulled to the curb and stopped.

Dev shoved some money at the man and stepped out, then helped Felicity to the sidewalk. "Nice address. I live a couple of blocks from here." He took her arm and led her up the two shallow steps to the door. "You remember my parents' place?"

"Yes." When she'd arrived at her apartment Wednesday evening, she'd been shocked to realize how close the Abramses' home was. She had wondered if she would be able to walk past it without painful memories assaulting her.

"We'll talk about your moving in later," Dev said as the doorman let them into the building.

They crossed the lobby side by side. When they entered the elevator, Felicity faced him.

"I'm called Madame dai Haaji because I am the widow of Haaji dai Haaji. He was the uncle of the present king, and was assassinated a year ago by religious fanatics opposed to the king."

Blood rushed from Dev's face, and his features seemed to turn to ice. "So." The word whistled between his lips like an uncoiled whip. "You married." Felicity had belonged to another man. When he had thought her dead, she had been lying in someone else's arms. Another man had touched her, loved her. . . . The blackness that had lain dormant exploded in his brain. His being retched in rejection; his mind fragmented; his soul froze. He struggled to find one shred of information that didn't cut into him. "He was a very important man in Dahrain, wasn't he? He helped establish the democratic government." His voice had a strange echoing sound to him, as though he were trapped in a bell.

"Yes." Felicity gulped in oxygen. Why didn't Dev react? Where was the volatility? Was he behind that icy mask? "Without Haaji, Esther and I would have died. He had come to Beirut on a peace mission and had heard an American woman and infant were being held hostage. He managed to get us released."

Dev ground his teeth. "And you married him

right away. Did you wait until the ink was dry on my death notice?"

"It wasn't like that!" She lowered her voice. "It wasn't like that."

The elevator doors opened onto a small rectangular foyer that fronted the penthouse apartment. Felicity crossed to the door and unlocked it. She felt as though the events of the last hour had unhinged every joint in her body. Her walk seemed out of sync, erratic. The smallest motion knocked her off balance.

She opened the door and turned to Dev. "I think—"

"I want to see my daughter."

"She's asleep."

"I won't wake her." He drew in a deep breath. "I called Pacer and told him you were here."

Felicity felt airy and happy all at once. For a time the gloom receded. "Is he com—" She was interrupted by a call on the intercom.

"Speak of the devil," Dev said icily. He'd noticed how her eyes brightened at the mention of his friend. Jealousy was not an emotion he was used to. Nor did he like it.

Felicity hurried into the apartment. "Yes?" she said into the intercom.

"Pacer Dillon to see you, ma'am," the doorman said.

"Oh, yes. Tell him to come up at once." She turned to Dev. "He's coming up."

"I heard," Dev said, swallowing the black bile.

Jealous of Pacer? He was losing his mind. His gaze swept over her. "You're still very beautiful."

"And you're still tougher than old boots." Her laugh was shaky. She had tried for so long to bury the pain of losing him, but she could never entirely forget him. Finding him again was agonizing and wondrous.

Someone rapped sharply on the door and Dev opened it. "Hi."

"Hi." Pacer grinned. "You look ready to bite through an oak tree."

"Go to hell," Dev said easily.

"Yeah, I read you too well. . . ." His voice died as he looked beyond his friend to Felicity. "Damn! It is you. I thought he was out of his mind again. He's been that way off and on since you . . . you . . . Felicity!" He strode past Dev and swept a laughing, crying Felicity into his arms.

Another sharp jolt of jealousy shook Dev. Not once in all the time he had known Pacer Creekwood Dillon had he ever felt anything but affection for him. But right now he could have punched his lights out.

Pacer was still holding Felicity when he glanced at Dev. His smile widened. "Going to kill me?"

"Maybe."

Pacer set Felicity on her feet again. "Back to life, are we, Dev?"

"Don't be cute, you damned giant. You don't have the credentials."

Pacer laughed outright as Felicity stared at Dev.

He stared back, and none of them heard the patter of feet down the hall.

"Mommy? You woke me. My teddy is asleep."

Felicity whirled around, startled by the sound of her daughter's voice. "Esther. You must go back to bed. It's very late." She started toward her child. So did Dev.

"I don't want you to call me Esther, Mommy," the girl said. "I want you to call me Suni like Daddy did."

Dev stopped dead, shuddering as though he'd been stabbed. Then he knelt in front of the child. "Esther is your grandmother's name."

"Oh. Did you know her?"

"Yes." He reached out a hand, but pulled it back when he saw wariness on her face. "Suni is a beautiful name, but would you mind if I called you Esther?"

Pacer hunkered down next to Dev, catching the girl's eyes. "And I would like to call you that too."

She nodded, then looked at her mother. "Will that be my name when I go to school?"

"Yes," Felicity whispered, tears stinging her eyes. Dev and Esther were so alike. The same strong bones, the same determined chin. They both had a way of cocking their heads to one side when mulling over something. It was a sublime happiness to see them together again, their dark, dark hair shining in the light.

Yet Felicity felt so confused. It had taken great effort to lock memories of Dev in the back of her mind. Facing him now, she felt as though a hurricane had blown through her life, disrupting it, changing everything.

He glanced up at her. "I want you to stay at my place tonight."

She shook her head.

"Then I'll stay here."

She opened her mouth to protest, then noted Esther's interested gaze. "Do what you wish. Come, dear, you must get to bed. You'll see everyone tomorrow."

Esther yawned. "Good night," she said to Dev and Pacer. "I'll see you tomorrow."

Felicity watched Dev as he rose to his feet, his body stiff, his gaze locked on Esther. Pain clutched her. All this time he had thought his daughter was dead. Now he saw her and had to hear her refer to another man as Daddy. She scooped up the child and carried her back down the hall to her bedroom.

"Dev?" Pacer said. "Dev, listen to me. The nightmare is over. You won't have the dreams anymore. She's back."

Dev looked at him blindly. "I hate to let her out of my sight."

"I know. I called Con and Heller. They can't believe it any more than I could." Pacer shook his head. "I needed to see her to believe it. Destiny brought you back together, Dev. It had to be."

Dev tried to smile at his friend. "That Indian mysticism of yours working overtime again?"

"You could say that."

For the first time Dev looked around the room. "Nice apartment."

"Thinking of buying the building?" Pacer teased. "You must have a little money left over from your last novel. Your war stories do well."

"Yeah." By writing fictionalized accounts of what had happened to him as an overseas correspondent in the war-torn sections of the world, Dev had been able to exorcise some of his ghosts. Only when he was writing, or "dabbling" in real estate, was he able to forget, for a time, the pain in his life.

"Shall I bring you a change of clothes tomorrow?" Pacer asked.

"I'll call Mrs. Aldebrand and have her send something over by messenger."

"Fine."

Pacer waited for Felicity to return, then said good night to them both. After he left, Felicity turned to Dev.

"You should go too, Dev. There's—"

"Do you have any food in this place? I missed my supper."

She stiffened. "The kitchen is this way."

"How long did you stay in Beirut after you were rescued?" he asked as he followed her.

"Not long. The fighting had begun in earnest, and Haaji's peace mission had failed."

She could still recall how ill she'd been. She had gone in and out of a fever for several weeks and barely remembered the trip to Dahrain. When she recovered, Haaji had offered her a choice. She could return to the States, or she could marry him. He had fallen in love with her.

She had grown fond of Haaji herself, and decided to stay. Her mother had died the previous year and she had no other relatives. Since she had traveled so much as a photographer for a news agency, she had no strong ties to any one place. And with Dev gone . . . Haaji had offered her a haven, and she had grabbed it.

She switched on the light in the kitchen. "Help yourself. I'm afraid there are only two bedrooms in the apartment. If you want to stay, you'll have to sleep on the couch."

"That's fine."

His intent stare was making her nervous, and she turned away. "I'll get you some linens."

She started back down the hall, but his soft voice stopped her. "I'm in your life to stay, Felicity. Accept that."

She glanced at him over her shoulder. His face revealed none of the warmth or tenderness the man she had loved had once lavished on her. Suppressing a shiver, she hurried away from him.

Two

Dev wasn't used to going to bed before the sun came up, and stretching out on the L-shaped couch in the living room wasn't exactly conducive to sleep. Years of prowling the caves of Manhattan nightlife had fixed a pattern in him. But there was no thought of leaving the apartment.

Finally, after he'd gone to the kitchen three times and the bathroom twice that many, his taut nerves uncoiled and he could close his eyes and sleep.

He should have known the dream would come. It often did when he was strung out emotionally. Nothing stopped the dream once it started. Even when his body was coated with sweat and he tossed fitfully, the dream was relentless. It carried him away.

It always began innocently, taking him back to when he'd been on a free-lance assignment in an African country torn apart by revolution. He had raced for a train out of the country, just ahead of a rebel army, with a female photographer from Reuters. If it hadn't been such a hell of a mess, if there hadn't been so many frightened people trying to jam onto the train, if he hadn't lost her in the crowd, he might have arranged to meet her somewhere. Too many ifs. He put her in the back pocket of his mind, but he didn't forget her.

The dream shifted to London, weeks later. He was in The Grill, a fine restaurant in one of the classiest hotels, feeling happy and at peace with himself. That day he had gotten a job with *World*, an international news magazine.

He had just taken his seat when he saw her crossing the room in his direction. His heart nose-dived and he stood up to intercept her.

"Hello again," he said. "You're looking better than the last time I saw you."

There was no recognition in her violet eyes as she stared at him. Without speaking, she stepped to one side to get around him. He put his hand on her arm to stop her.

"Wait," he said. "Don't you remember—"

"No, I don't," she said in a low voice. "And I'm not interested."

Unconsciously, he tightened his grip on her arm. "But—"

Swiftly and discreetly, she kicked him in the shin. The sudden pain caused him to release her, and she strode away. "Remember *that*," she tossed over her shoulder.

Still in a foul mood, he returned to his hotel

late that night. His phone rang a few minutes later.

"This is Felicity Dobbs," the woman on the other end said. "Ah . . . I'm the one who kicked you at The Grill tonight."

"I remember."

"Sorry. I didn't realize that we'd met . . . that you were who you were. The person I was eating with told me who you were and I recognized the name and that we'd met in Africa last month. I'm babbling. What I want to do is apologize."

"I'll accept only if you have dinner with me. And if you promise to keep your feet to yourself."

Her low chuckle came through the phone like a kiss. Dev felt the first heart fluttering of his life.

They married and it was good. *World* wanted him to cover the Middle East, and he accepted the assignment primarily because Felicity was able to get one there as well.

Then the horror began. The dream turned to nightmare and Dev couldn't stop it.

The shouting woke Felicity. She ran into the living room and saw Dev thrashing on the couch. "Dev! Dev, wake up."

He sat up wild-eyed, staring at her as though she were a ghost. Then he sagged and shook his head. "Sorry. Nightmare. What did I say?"

"You kept yelling, 'No, no.!' I didn't understand the rest of it. Can I get you something? A hot drink maybe?"

So Dev had bad dreams too, she thought. How ironic. What would he say if she told him about the tortures in her mind, the sleepwalking, the tears on her face when she wakened. Yet not once had she been able to recall any of the dreams.

Dev threw off the comforter that had tangled around his body. "There's a lot you can do for me," he said as he stood. "A hot drink isn't one of them."

She ignored his provocative remark. "It will help you sleep."

"I'm not interested in sleep right now." He gazed at her greedily, wanting that satin-clad body pressed to his. Slowly, he walked toward her. "You look beautiful in pink. Exciting, ready for love."

Her thighs seemed to melt, despite her best efforts to resist his seductive voice. "It's just past dawn," she said wearily. She couldn't tear her gaze from him. Except for very brief boxer shorts, he was naked. And he was magnificent. Whatever he'd been doing these past several years, he still looked like Apollo. "Ah, I should get back to bed."

"Me too. This couch isn't that comfortable." He grinned when he saw her chin come up, her eyes narrow. "Going to offer me half of your bed?"

"No."

He shrugged. "I'll settle for the hot drink, then."

He was still moving toward her. As he neared he seemed to electrify the air. She couldn't draw enough oxygen into her lungs. Would he have to breathe into her mouth so she could function? She felt like a helium balloon, rising, rising, out of control. Yet . . . Dev could reach her.

She turned on her heel and strode from the room.

"Running?"

"Not at all," she called back. "You said you wanted a hot drink."

"So I did."

She had to smother the desire to gallop away from him. Damn him! He'd always been able to dredge up anger and love from her, even at the same time. She considered herself a calm person . . . but not around Dev.

The kitchen was small but functional, and Dev swallowed all the space. It was hard to get around him. He didn't try to make himself scarce, either. Had he kissed her neck when she'd just passed him? Goose bumps the size of eggs were rising on her skin. That man could ruin her health. How deluded she had been when they were married. She'd felt energized all the time. Actually, he had probably begun destroying her health even then.

She glared at him as he blocked her way to the sink. "Excuse me."

"Of course. Let me help." His arms slid around her from behind as she filled the kettle. "I could wash some lettuce if you'd like a sandwich."

"Don't eat at night."

"Are you getting a cold? Your voice sounds husky."

"You can't intimidate me, Dev Abrams." She twisted around in his hold until her back was pressed against the sink.

"Why would a sandwich intimidate you?" His

leg slid so naturally between hers. "Just trying to balance myself."

"Now whose voice is hoarse?"

"You've always had the power to knock me out, darling. No one ever could arouse me more."

He leaned down and pressed his mouth to her neck, closing his eyes as he inhaled the very special fragrance that was Felicity's alone. Even doing that was invigorating, arousing. How dead he'd been without her.

"I won't be just another woman in your life," she said, though she didn't push him away.

"You were always the only woman in my life."

"I'm not blind. I got a glimpse of those two leggy twits who were at the theater with you."

"I didn't marry them." He nibbled the tender flesh at the corner of her mouth.

"Don't bite me."

"Why not? You sliced, diced, and cubed me and thought nothing of it."

"That's not true. You were dead, Dev. I was trying to save our daughter and myself, and I did." She tried to pull away from him, but it only made the sink dig into her back.

He tightened his arms. "Let's table this discussion for now. Kiss me, Felicity."

She was going to tell him to go to hell. Instead, she lifted her head, giving him access to her mouth.

When her lips touched his, he thought his heart would burst. Felicity! How he'd needed her. Kissing her was a lifeline! He hadn't even realized he was a zombie until her tongue touched his and blood roared through his veins. He held her even closer as though he would pull her inside himself, make her a part of him forever.

Home! Felicity thought. Dev was an exciting homecoming that nothing else could match. He was fireworks and peace, excitement and contentment. He was all of life and more. When she thought he was pulling back from her, she groaned softly.

"Easy, darling, I'm just getting us more comfortable."

She again pressed her mouth to his, seeking the solace, the passion, she'd thought lost to her. She would deal with the realities later. Now, she needed Dev.

"Felicity . . ." Dev's entire body trembled in response when her mouth opened under his, her hands digging into him in remembered ecstasy.

"Mommy, what are you doing? The sun is shining in my room and I'm hungry."

"Wha'zat?" Dev stared down at Felicity when she pulled back from him. The childish voice barely penetrated the thundering passion building in him.

"Esther," Felicity said shakily.

He turned, his eyes widening when he saw his daughter gazing seriously at him, a slight frown on her face. "Hi," he said. "Mommy was going to make me a hot drink."

"Oh. Why are you here so early in the morning? Where are your clothes?"

Not in many years had Dev felt at such a loss for words. "Uh, you see, I slept here last night, Esther, on the couch."

"Oh. Are you making breakfast, Mommy?"

"Well, it's early," Felicity said, "but I suppose I could make us something. Why don't you go back to your room and get your slippers. They'll keep your feet warm and then you can help me."

Esther shot one more glance at Dev, then left.

Dev looked down at Felicity. "Don't regret what happened. It was real and right."

"Esther shouldn't have seen us like that," she said lamely.

"That's not true and you know it. She should see more of that. I'm not getting out of your life, Felicity."

"It's been nearly six years. We've both changed so much. What if we can't work out the differences?"

"Then we'll trash what we had," he said harshly, furious that she was being so negative. "Either way, I'm not getting out of my daughter's life."

Felicity moved away from him and opened the refrigerator. "Perhaps you'll want to put on your clothes for breakfast."

"The discussion isn't over, Felicity." He slammed out of the kitchen, banging his toe against the door when he kicked it and muttering curses all the way back to the living room.

Later that morning, Dev was back in his brownstone. If he hadn't convinced Felicity to come and live with him right away, at least she hadn't closed the door on the idea.

He dialed a number and waited. "Wellington? Dev. No, I'm not coming back to work for *World*. Could you do something for me? I need everything you have on Haaji dai Haaji. That's right, the Dahrainian king's uncle. Could you get back to me as soon as you can? Great. Thanks."

He replaced the receiver, stared at it for a moment, then dialed once more. "Heller? It's Dev."

"Oh, Dev, Dev, I can't believe it. Pacer called us. You know how stoical he is, but I thought he was going to cry."

"I felt a little teary myself. I was wondering if you and Con would join us for an early dinner this evening. Here. I thought if you brought the children, they could get to know Esther."

"Consider it done. You know I love Mrs. Aldebrand's cooking. Should I call Pacer?"

"I think he'll be here this morning. I'll talk to him then."

"Dev, I'm a little nervous . . ."

"You're perfect. Felicity will love you and vice versa. See you tonight."

He hung up and walked to his bathroom to shower and change. Tonight he would have the people he loved under his roof, all of them.

Felicity stared out her bedroom window. It was so unreal. Dev was alive. He was in New York only a couple of blocks away. She would see him again today . . . and maybe every day from here on. Fantasy! But not even the wonder of it all could wipe away the fact that she and Dev had changed, that their time apart had formed two different people. Could she deal with that? Could he?

Memory cascaded her back to those days in Beirut. Happiness had been the order of the day. She and Dev had managed their schedules so they had the most time possible together. Not even the war that was tearing Beirut apart intruded on the beautiful mystique that was theirs.

When she had lost Dev, she had thought she would never survive. But she had. Now her priorities were different: her life was centered on her child. But, then, in the beginning . . .

Lovemaking had been a constant with them. When they were together they created their own world, shutting out the bleak reality of Beirut.

"I'm starved for you, Felicity. I haven't seen you in aeons."

"You saw me this morning at breakfast, my sexy husband."

"Make love to me, Felicity."

When the doorbell rang, it took Felicity a moment to orient herself. Hadn't she just been in Beirut? In Dev's arms?

She walked to the door, calling, "Who is it?"

"It's Pacer, Felicity."

She threw open the door and stepped into his warm embrace. "Hello. It's so good to see you."

He looked down at her thoughtfully. "I have to talk to you."

She studied him. Pacer had always been the most taciturn of the trio of friends. "Come in."

They walked into the living room and sat down opposite each other.

"Is something wrong with Dev?" she asked.

Pacer looked up, startled. "No, no, darlin', it's not like that." He sighed and sat back. "I don't think you know the Dev Abrams you see."

"He's harder."

"Much. But it's more than that. After he came back from Beirut, he was a madman." Pacer sat forward, his hands linked between his knees. "He didn't care about anything. If he got hold of money, he would take a ridiculous chance with it, wanting to lose, even seeming a little disappointed when a crazy, long-shot deal worked out. And they usually did. He started to make money, his gambling and carelessness turning to gold. But nothing gave him peace or satisfaction. He was crazy."

"Lots of women?"

"Yes." Pacer shook his head. "You had to see him. Not even in 'Nam had I ever seen him that way. He was an out-of-control rocket, ready to explode, to kill or maim anything or anyone in his way." Pacer stared hard at her. "Life ceased for him, Felicity. He wouldn't even talk to Wellington about continuing his job. Fortunately, Wellington let him out of the contract. Then he started buying property. Broken-down buildings, ghetto lots that he would build on, stretching himself, going out on a limb . . . trying to go broke."

"He never was a money man, so it wouldn't matter to him if he went broke."

Pacer nodded. "But he couldn't lose." He laughed softly. "The more money he made, the crazier he got. Con and I were scared at times. He alienated everyone except us. He partied every night and never slept."

"Nightmares."

"You know?"

"He had one last night. I heard him just before dawn. He thrashed around on the couch like a demented person."

Pacer shrugged. "I suppose that's one of the reasons he still doesn't like to go to sleep." His smile was twisted. "I don't know if I would have let you near him the way he was. . . ."

"Thank you, Pacer, for telling me this."

"I know it's going to be difficult for you, but I'm here for you as well as Dev, and so is Con. And wait until you meet Heller."

"Dev told me she's beautiful."

"Inside and out, and their children are the best. Dev and I are godfathers to them."

"I've never seen you beam before, Pacer Creekwood Dillon."

"I'm godfather to Esther too," he said softly. He stood and pulled her up into his arms. "And I'm your friend, lady."

"I know." She rested her forehead on his chest for a moment.

• • •

"Dev? It's Wellington. I got quite a bit of information on dai Haaji. He was mucho importante, amigo. Not only was he the uncle of the young king, he was also his most trusted adviser. And head of security."

"What about his death?"

"Assassination by a right-wing faction that is trying to overthrow the king and the fledgling democratic government, and establish a religious government like they have in Iran. So tell me, Dev. Why are you so interested in dai Haaji?"

He couldn't tell Wellington the truth. It was ridiculous, crazy even, to be jealous of a dead man. A man who had saved the life of his wife and daughter. "I can't say much right now, Wellington."

"Sounds mysterious. But, Dev, if it turns into a good story . . ."

"It's yours. Tell me about the Dahrainian government now. Is it stable?"

"I think so. In fact, King Ahmed is coming to this country in a few weeks. Would you like to cover it?"

"No. Why is he coming?"

"Ah, let's see, here it is. He's speaking at an oil producers' seminar right here in Manhattan. Looks uncomplicated."

"Fine. Let me know if anything comes across your desk that seems out of the ordinary."

"Sure, Dev. Wish you would change your mind about coming with us again."

"I won't."

"All right, I guess I'll have to accept that. Well, I'll be in touch."

"Wellington. Wait. There's something you should know. Felicity is back."

"Felicity who?"

"My wife."

"That can't be. She's dead."

"She's alive, and she and our daughter have been in Dahrain. She's right here in New York."

"Dammit, you're kidding! My God, I could cry. It's wonderful. All that pain you went through is over now."

"Yes." Dev wished that were true. An idea occurred to him, and without bothering to think it through, he voiced it. "I'm thinking of giving a party for Felicity . . . before we go to my place upstate. Probably in a week. I hope you'll come."

"Wouldn't miss it. And taking your wife and daughter to the mountains could be just the thing for them."

"Yes." If Felicity would come, if Esther could be persuaded. Dammit! They needed the time alone to sort things out. Surely she would see that. "Good-bye, Wellington. I'll let you know when the party is."

"Mommy? Where are you?" Esther bounced into her mother's bedroom and stopped dead. "Why have you pushed your face against the window?"

"Ah .. . it feels cool." She turned her head and smiled at her daughter, thinking, not for the first time, how stilted and British her English sounded. Though the child had been taught Dahrainian and spoke it fluently, her nurses and guards had been encouraged to speak with her in English and French as well. So she spoke it at times with an accent. She sometimes used English idioms rather than American. "I was just thinking."

"Where's that man?"

Felicity inhaled deeply and smiled at her beloved child. "Come and sit down, love. I want to talk to you."

Esther didn't move, her head shaking slowly. "Is he my father who was dead?"

Felicity sighed. "You heard us talking." At her daughter's nod, she smiled sadly. Dev's daughter had the same purposeful glint in her eye as her father always had. "Yes. It was someone else who died in prison, not Daddy, but they gave out his name; that's why we thought the wrong thing."

"I liked my Daddy Haaji."

"I know. So did I. But he's gone now and we should try to be fair with your real daddy. He wants to be near you. He loves you."

Esther looked thoughtful. "I don't think he's bad."

Felicity smiled and held out her arms. "That's a start."

"Does he want us to stay with him?" Esther asked from the safety of her mother's embrace.

"Yes, I think he would like that."

"Does he have horses like we did in Dahrain? I like horses."

"Well, why don't you ask him that?"

"I will."

• • •

Dev stared at the phone, then dialed. "Con? Dev. Yeah, it's great. I can't get used to it." He cleared his throat. "I've just talked to Wellington and gotten some background on Haaji dai Haaji."

"Pacer told me Felicity married him after she'd been told you were dead."

"Yes. She left Beirut before anyone could tell her I was alive."

"Easy, man. Be realistic, Dev. We both know that information in the Middle East gets garbled at best, lost at worst. Obviously, rumors of her death were greatly exaggerated too."

"I know, I know."

"You're raw, Dev, with great open sores. It will take time to treat each one."

"I know you're right and I agree with you . . . but I've never been so floored in my life."

"I understand. Do you want me to put out some feelers and see what I can find out about dai Haaji?"

"You're a perceptive guy, old buddy."

"Consider it done. When are we going to see her?"

"I just decided when I was talking to Wellington to have a welcome-home party here, probably next week. But I know she'd like to see you and your family before that, so I called Heller about dinner tonight."

"And we will be there. I'm sure Heller told you that."

"She did. Thanks, Con."

"Dev. Take it slow, talk to her."

"Right."

When Dev hung up the phone, it rang almost immediately. "Dev Abrams."

"Dev, it's Felicity. We didn't discuss when we'd see each other today, and . . . well, I think Esther should get to know you. So, I wondered if you'd like to come to dinner tonight, here at the apartment."

A little tension eased from Dev. Thank heavens she was making an overture toward him. Now he just hoped she wouldn't mind that he'd already made plans for all of them.

"I'd love to have dinner with you and Esther," he said. "But actually, I was hoping you two could come over here. I've invited Pacer and Con and Heller and their children already."

She was silent for a moment, then she muttered, "Still trying to run my life, Abrams? Some things never change." Her voice lightened. "But that's all right. I'm eager to see Con again, and to meet his wife. And it will be good for Esther to meet other children."

Dev sighed silently with relief. "That's what I thought. Why don't I come by now to get you?"

"Fine. I'll see you in a few minutes."

After warning his housekeeper, Mrs. Aldebrand, about his dinner guests, Dev headed for Felicity's apartment. Since it was such a short distance away, he walked, enjoying the warm, sunny day. Besides, with Manhattan traffic as bad as always, it probably would have taken him longer to drive.

When he reached the building he was surprised to see a man in a security uniform standing in front of it.

"I didn't notice any security guards when I was here last night," he said easily when the man stopped him.

"Melson Security, sir. There was an attempted burglary early this morning and we've been hired by the Dahrainian consulate to protect the premises. We'll be checking everyone who comes in, sir."

"Fine." Dev gave his name and showed identification. The doorman told him he was expected, and he went straight upstairs. When he got off the elevator, she was waiting for him at her door.

"I understand someone tried to break in here today," he said as they stepped into the apartment.

She nodded. "It must have been about the time you left this morning. I didn't even know about it until security called. I'm not sure which apartment was involved . . . Dev?"

He pulled her into his arms and his mouth came down on hers with gentle fierceness. He urged her lips to part, then slipped his tongue between them. The kiss went on, firing them, melding them. When he lifted his head, his breathing was harsh, uneven. "I don't want you to stay here. It could be dangerous."

"Dev." She could see the hot anxiety in him, like an open wound. "It's all right. It didn't involve us."

He bent his head so his forehead was touching

hers. "Stay at my place. I want you there. You'll be safe."

His feverish urgency communicated itself to her. His blood pumped through his skin to her. Moving closer, she put her arms around his neck, her eyes closing in the quiet ecstasy that she thought she'd never know again.

"You are always holding my mommy." Esther had come out of her bedroom and was staring at Dev. "My mommy says you're my other father."

Dev released Felicity and knelt in front of his daughter, nodding his head. "Will you give me a kiss too?"

Esther smiled shyly and moved closer.

Her small hand touching his face delighted him so much, he felt teary. Her mouth against his check seared him for all time. His beautiful child. "I'd like you to come and stay in my house, Esther," he said huskily.

"Do you have horses? Mommy said I could ask you."

He chuckled. "I don't have them in Manhattan, but we could go up to my place in the mountains. I have some there."

"I'd like that."

Esther laughed delightedly, and Dev felt as if he'd been poleaxed. He picked up her hand and kissed the back of it. "I would like that too. Shall we go? You and Mommy are going to have dinner at my place tonight."

"Yes, I know. I'm going to bring Roscoe. He's my teddy bear."

Dev was dazed by the power Esther had over him. When she skipped back down the hall he rose and looked at Felicity. "She's as beautiful as her mother."

Felicity's heart fluttered with a girlish joy. She could have laughed out loud like Esther. "Thank you."

"I mean it." He walked back to her and brushed his mouth across her cheek. "You excite me more each time I see you."

She pressed a hand to his jaw, and a lightning bolt seemed to shoot through her. "You generate some heat yourself."

"Do I?"

Though there was space between them, she felt their bodies must be fused, their hearts and lungs functioning as one.

"In all things that matter, Felicity Dobbs Abrams, I'm yours."

"Those were the vows we wrote for our wedding," she said, her voice shaking.

"Yes."

"Our wedding was so beautiful."

"Don't cry, love." He caught on his finger the tear that slipped down her cheek.

"Is it too far-gone, Dev? Can it come back?"

"It was never lost, Felicity," he said fiercely, and kissed her once more.

"You're doing it again," Esther said interestedly. "Do you like to do that?"

Dev lifted his head and stared at his child. "Very much. I could kiss your mommy all day, every day, and never get tired. And I could do the same to you."

Esther giggled. "That's silly."

"Uh-uh. Come here." He laughed as he swept her up into his arms, and kissed her cheek again and again. When her small arms circled his neck, he knew he had never felt such joy before.

Felicity saw the wonder on Dev's face and happiness flooded her. There could be a chance for them.

Dev set Esther down. "I've decided to have a party to welcome you home. You can tell me what you think on the way to my place. Let's go, ladies."

Felicity smiled blindingly at him. "Already I think it's a wonderful idea."

He leaned close to her. "I haven't seen that smile since the last time we were in bed, darling. You've aroused me." He grinned when her face reddened.

"As I recall, it never took much," she said tartly.

"You remember correctly," he murmured as he followed her to the door.

Three

Manhattan put on her best face for the party the following Saturday night. It was unseasonably balmy for autumn in New York. The sky was a gray silk that would darken to ebony with a smattering of diamonds cast across it.

Guests started arriving at eight and continued streaming in until it seemed the brownstone could hold no more. At the center of the glittering, whirling crowd was Felicity. And Dev couldn't take his eyes off her.

"I don't often see him calf-eyed, do you, Con?" Pacer said idly, then grinned when Dev whirled to face him.

Con laughed. "The beautiful lady has knocked him out."

"'What's so amusing?" Dev asked. "You've been on another planet since you met Heller." He smiled when his friend winced and said "Guilty."

"I think both women would prefer me," Pacer drawled. "Maybe I'll make a run for the roses."

"He has a death wish, Con."

"No doubt."

Ione, Con's sister, sailed up to them. "What are the three of you hatching?" She kissed Dev on the cheek. "She's fabulous, Dev, darling. That dress is haute couture, of course. Did she buy it in Paris? Not many women would dare wear that shade of violet. It just matches her eyes. Oh, dear, there's someone I must see."

Dev stared across the room at Felicity, who was talking to Melanie Wendel, Con's mother. "There's someone I must see too," he muttered, and strode away.

Pacer shot a glance at Con. "Why are you chuckling, old chum?"

"My guess is that he didn't buy Felicity's dress. That would irk him some."

"Yeah, I guess it would. I know dai Haaji was a wealthy man. And Felicity has great style. He probably wanted her to dress well."

"Speaking of dai Haaji," Con said abruptly.

"Were we?" Pacer was alert, though his indolent stance hadn't altered.

"We are now. He was a man with many enemies. He spent a great deal of time and effort trying to establish the democratic government of Dahrain, and the rest of the time dodging assassins. There had been numerous attempts on his life before the one that killed him."

Pacer shifted slightly. There was an indefinable readiness about him. "And?"

Con shrugged, seeming uncomfortable. "Nothing, really."

"I read you. You've got an insect bite on that brain of yours."

"Something like that."

Pacer took a deep breath. "Did you know there was an attempted burglary in the building where Felicity was staying?"

Con straightened. "Isn't there usually a house guard at places used by foreign countries?"

"Dev asked the same question."

"I see."

Dev smiled at Melanie Wendel. "Yes, I'm glad she's here. She and Esther moved in on Thursday. They both like this house, and there's more room here than there was at her apartment."

"And you need them here." Melanie squeezed his hand. "After you and she have some time together, I'll want to have lunch with her, just the two of us so that we can catch up with what's happened these last few years."

"I'm sure Felicity would love to have lunch with you anytime." His gaze slid toward Felicity, who now stood a short distance away talking to Wellington Ford. "But I want to take her and our daughter to the mountains. You're right. The three of us need time together."

"Of course you do." Melanie kissed his cheek. "We're all so happy for you."

"I know. Thank you." He hugged the woman who had been as supportive as his own mother, and whom he loved almost as much as he had loved his parents.

When a friend came up to speak to Melanie, she excused herself. Dev strolled over to Felicity, waiting until someone gained Wellington's attention.

"You look beautiful," he whispered in her ear. "That swath of violet silk clings to your body the way I want to."

"Lecher," she said feebly, reacting as always to his presence. The fine hairs on her body were standing up straight as though an electric charge had just jolted through her. Had she levitated? She shot a glance at her pumps. No, she was still on the floor. When she gazed back at Dev, her heart flip-flopped. "Dev, stop looking at me that way."

"Your nipples are hardening under that dress, aren't they, darling? I can tell because I'm having a similar response. Have I told you how much I love having you here?"

"This house was a favorite with your parents too." Her gaze flowed over him. He looked sexy and gorgeous in his midnight blue evening suit. Dev was lethal to any woman. It made her want to preen that he desired her.

"Yes," he said. "You remembered."

"I remember a great many things."

"Do you, darling?"

"Dev, don't." All at once she felt breathless. "That bedroom look will shock your guests."

"Let's tell them to go home."

"We can't do that." Why didn't all the guests leave? "We should dance . . . or something."

"Fine." He took her hand and led her from the living room into the solarium, whose three glass walls were mantled in greenery and flowers. The Persian carpets had been pushed aside and a small band in one corner played softly.

Taking her in his arms, he closed his eyes and inhaled. "Is that Joy perfume?"

"Yes." Anger fountained in her for a moment. When had Dev become a connoiseur of perfumes?

"Umm, darling, you're digging your nails into me. I love it, even though I think it's from temper, not passion."

"Right."

"The remark about the perfume?"

Dev had always been able to read her too well, she thought. "You must have fine-tuned your knowledge of women these last years," she snapped.

"Darling, how you talk." He whirled her away from his body, gyrating to the now-fast beat. "You could always move."

"So could you." The music seemed to release Felicity. She felt free, unfettered, cut loose from earth and its cares. Lifting her arms in a primeval gesture to the moon, she swayed and whirled to the music as though the gods dictated the tune.

Heller Wendel turned to her husband. "They are wildly beautiful together, aren't they?"

Con tightened his arm around her waist. "I used to think that I understood Dev's pain, but I didn't really, not until I met you and almost lost you." He gazed at his beloved wife. "No wonder he was a zombie."

"Sweetheart." She smiled at him. "I don't suppose we could leave early."

"We certainly can," he said promptly, loving the sensuality in her smile.

Throughout the night Felicity danced with nearly every man there, yet when each dance ended, Dev claimed her for the next one. "Shouldn't you be dancing with some of your female guests?" she asked him at one point.

"I let Pacer do that."

She laughed. "He's shy."

"Is he? If you could have seen him in Vietnam when he dismantled a dozen guards to get to Con's cell, then literally tore out the bars with his hands, you wouldn't call him shy. He's a veritable devil when he's fired up."

"I mean with women."

"I think Pace could handle himself in any situation. He's complex, fearless, and dangerous in a fight." Dev smiled. "I would hate to be the woman he finally sets his heart on. He can burn white-hot."

"I don't expect him to fight women."

"Why not? I've had to fight you on occasion."

Felicity was silent for a moment. Despite the joy of being with Dev again, of seeing him with their daughter, she still worried the differences between

them were too great to be overcome. "There could
be more fighting," she said.

"All marriages have disagreements, problems."

She stopped dancing. "Maybe we could walk in
the garden."

"Fine." Dev felt a sudden, prickling wariness.
With his hand at the small of her back, he guided
her through the French doors that led to the small
courtyard in the back. When they hit a patch of
darkness he turned her to him. "Kiss me."

"Dev, I didn't come out here to—"

"I know. But I need the kiss."

"I need it, too, come to think of it," she muttered, and pressed her mouth to his. Her body
was pliant in his arms, needing him. She wanted
nothing more than to be his, to love him and hold
him forever. Realization was both wonder and
pain. Dev was all of life to her. That hadn't
changed.

Tongue touched tongue, and the world exploded
in the passion they'd always been able to build with
each other, time after time.

"Darling! I need you." Dev was caught in the
maelstrom of desire. Feeling her body against his
was whirling him out of control. "Whatever else is
in front of us, Felicity, we have a power between
us."

"Dev." Out of breath, feeling as though she'd
spun through space, Felicity pushed back from
him. "There are complications that need talking
out, Dev. We have to feel our way on this. I'm
older; so are you. Our outlooks on many things

have shifted. We've lived different lives for the past five years."

"This isn't news to me."

"You're biting through steel."

"You used to tell me that when we argued."

"We had verbal battles, not arguments."

"But we knew how to make up."

Felicity didn't smile. "Now we have a daughter. We don't have the space to let fly when we choose. Before we decide if we're going to . . . stay together, we'll have to settle many of our differences. We need to provide a stable, calm home for Esther."

"I'll buy that."

"Good."

"When do we start?"

"Ah, maybe tomorrow we could talk—"

"Why don't we go up to my place in the Catskills? We could talk there. Space, quiet, privacy. What do you think?"

"Maybe that would be best. When did you buy this place?"

"A couple of years ago, after I scored big on some property I sold."

He didn't mention that both Pacer and Con had gone through the roof when they'd seen the property, a block of broken-down, vacant apartment buildings in the Bronx. He had had a vague notion of renovating the buildings, turning them into safe, clean, affordable apartments, but it still had been a kamikaze venture. He had wanted to go broke, to sting himself. Yet his renovation idea had taken off, and he'd sold the property at enormous profit. He'd repeated the long shots, and the booze he consumed from morning till evening hadn't aided his thought processes. An errant fate kept him from losing, though, and more than once he had shaken his fists at the heavens.

"What are you thinking?" She touched his arm. "I see pain in your eyes."

"You should have seen me when I was told you were dead," he said quietly. "I was a madman."

"I went out of my mind when I heard you'd been executed. Only Esther kept me from going over the edge permanently."

"It was just a stroke of luck I never landed in jail." The words spilled from him like hot coals from a tipped brazier. "I did stupid things, dangerous things, so I could forget I was the one who'd put you in jeopardy by taking you to the Middle East."

"You couldn't have made me stay in London, Dev. I would have followed you anywhere. You know that."

"Yes. But it didn't lessen the pain of knowing you wouldn't have been in danger if you hadn't been with me." He lightly stroked her cheek. "I was wound pretty tight."

She loved his reluctant smile. It feathered over her like a caress. "Tell me what happened to you in Tehran."

Dev shrugged. "We—Eddie Baron, my photographer, and I—we were covering a rally, a religious gathering, where the spokesmen for the Ayatollah harangued the people. All at once there was some pushing; people surrounded us and screamed curses at us. We were arrested." He shook his head. "I can't tell you how awful it was. They accused me of being a spy, kept trying to force me to confess, kept threatening to execute me. Some days the only thing that kept me going was the thought of you and Esther. I thanked God you hadn't come with me. Then, to go back to Beirut and find out you were missing . . . to see your wedding ring on a woman's body . . ." He looked at her. "But you're alive. It's incredible."

"I know the feeling. Haaji had good information sources, but he never heard that you were actually alive. If I had known . . ." She shook her head. "But since my mother had died and you were gone, I had no reason to return home."

"I can understand that."

"Wellington said that you refused every offer of a job as a correspondent."

He nodded. "I hated the job after . . ."

She watched the play of light over his sharply carved features. "Sometimes . . . it's as though it happened to someone else, or that I dreamed it."

"I know how you feel. Dreams can be devastating."

"And that's why you stay awake all night and sleep in the daytime."

"I did. But I'm changing."

She chuckled. "It's either that or keep Esther up all night." She inhaled deeply when his smile seemed to flow over her again.

"Something like that."

Neither heard the French doors open behind them.

"Hey, you two, you have guests."

"Get lost, Pacer," Dev said softly, not turning.

"Can't. Mrs. W. sent me out here to get you. The ice carving on the buffet is melting."

Dev could hear the laughter in his friend's voice and spun around. "Who the hell cares if it turns into a flood?"

Felicity joined Pacer in his laughter. "He's still a barbarian, isn't he, Pacer?"

"Only you made the difference, darling," Dev murmured as he followed her into the house.

"Oh, there you are, Dev. Noodling in the garden?" Con's sister grinned cheekily at Dev, then smiled at Felicity. "He's a devil, you know, but I'm glad you love him. He's needed you. Shall we attack the buffet?"

"As Felicity walked away with Ione, she heard Dev murmur, "Don't be gone too long, love." She looked over her shoulder at him and caught the hot devilish look in his eyes. Delight shivered through her. God! Did he know the power he generated?

As they were seeing the last guests out, Dev stayed close to Felicity. She welcomed his touch. It was both comforting and exciting to have him beside her, his hand at her waist. But when he closed the door and they were at last alone, she suddenly felt nervous. She walked back into the living room and began to clean up.

"It's nice to be at a gathering where no one smokes," she said when she noticed him watching her.

"People don't smoke socially anymore unless they ask permission. It's considered bad form." He took the dishes from her and set them back down. "Mrs. Aldebrand will do it."

"It doesn't hurt to save her some steps."

"Why do you sound out of breath?"

"I don't."

He put his hands on her shoulders. "I want you and need you. Taking you to bed would be the fulfillment of my wildest fantasies. But nothing will happen between us unless you want it, love."

"I know." What would he say if she told him it wasn't he she was unsure of? That all her resolve to keep distance between them turned to jelly every time he looked at her? That she wasn't in control of her own feelings and reactions? She knew that if he kissed her right now, she would beg him to take her to bed.

"What is it?" he asked. "Headache? You're rubbing your temples."

"A bit of one." It was true. She did feel the strain of not pitching herself into his arms. She picked up the dirty plates again and carried them to the kitchen.

Dev followed with a tray of glasses. "You told me you were ill when you went to Dahrain. Did you have good care?"

"The best. Esther and I were always well cared for. Much of the time we lived in a small palace and there was an army of people to handle every need."

At first, though, her sorrow at losing Dev would overcome her and she would weep, alone, quietly, with no hope of assuaging the grief. Then one day she decided she would always grieve for Dev, always have an emptiness in her soul that she would have to learn to deal with in order to find and give happiness again. That day she began to smile, to enjoy her daughter, to take an interest in the people around her.

"I see." Dev was wrenched by ambivalent feelings. He was glad she and Esther had been well cared for. In fact, that washed away much of the pain he'd carried for so long. But . . . another man had provided for them. Another man had made love to her. . . . That cut like a knife. Yet he could live with it, as long as she was with him. Her presence was the balm his spirit, heart, and body needed. With Felicity alive and well, the problems would sort themselves out some way.

They made several trips back and forth to the kitchen, loaded the dishwasher, wiped up. But even doing the mundane chores didn't lessen the fierce electricity between them. It crackled like a live wire with every movement.

Felicity had trouble inhaling at times.

Dev felt as though flames licked along his veins.

At last they were finished.

"Mrs. Aldebrand will probably have a snit," Dev

said. "I don't usually enter her domain unless I want a snack."

"My lord sultan, how you have demeaned yourself." Felicity made an Arabian obeisance. When she saw his sapphire eyes narrow and glint, she yelped and sprinted for the door.

"You'd better run," Dev called, chasing after her. Her glorious legs, which had been a satin manacle to his body more than once, carried her gracefully up the stairs two at a time. "Darling, you really excite me," he murmured to himself as he stayed right behind her.

Felicity was sure she'd won. She was almost at the door to the master suite, which Dev had given her to use, her hand reaching for the knob. Success!

Strong arms caught her around the waist, and she gasped in surprise and protest.

"Gotcha!"

Laughing helplessly, she tried to turn and thump his chest, but her body was limp. When was the last time she'd let herself go in laughter, been overcome by mirth, played like a girl? She remembered exactly. She had been living with Dev, Esther was one and a half months old, and she'd insisted on having sex, though he'd been afraid to touch her.

Memory flooded her. How they'd laughed with joy at everything the infant Esther did. The three of them were often together on their big bed, the baby in the middle. Dev never tired of watching her nurse Esther.

"Will you promise to nurse me after our little girl moves on to other food?" he asked that evening.

She looked up at him. "You know I will. I want you very much."

He closed his eyes as if in pain. "Why did I start this conversation?"

"I don't know. Are you a masochist?"

He groaned and kissed her. "I must be."

She laughed delightedly, confident that she was loved. Soon Esther fell asleep in her arms. After she'd laid the baby in her crib, she returned to Dev, still lying on the bed. They teased each other and laughed, touched and kissed. In minutes the need that was always just below the surface erupted between them. Kisses were hot and deep; embraces were fierce and clinging.

Dev had backed off, moving away from her.

"Come over here and kiss me, fool," she'd said. "I've been starved for you."

"Oh, darling. Are you sure?"

"I'm sure. And I insist," she'd murmured throatily. Her heart soared when he'd capitulated with a groan.

It was as though they'd been parted for years, not mere weeks. The intimacy they shared had exploded over them, brand-new, untouched, wonderful.

Felicity trembled at the memory, needing Dev more now than she had that day many years ago.

"Hey, hey. Where are you, Felicity? You shivered."

Dev's question brought her back to the present with a vengeance. "What? Oh, I guess I was daydreaming."

"At midnight? That must be some day-dream."

"Ah . . . good night, Dev."

"Kiss me."

She inhaled deeply, a million reasons for saying no tumbling through her mind. Not the least of those was keeping her sanity. Then she stepped into his embrace, coiling her arms around his neck, pressing her legs against his sinewed thighs, her mouth open beneath his. All the passion, memory, and frustration funneled into one stunning kiss. It went on and on, deepening, tying them together, committing body and soul, burning bridges, dismantling barriers.

Somehow, Felicity found the strength to step back, her hands pressed to his chest. "Good night." The words were forced from her. All she wanted was to love him . . . but there was too much to talk about, discuss. Sex was a wonderful diversion, but it wasn't the answer.

His eyes still glazed with desire, he stared at her. "What?"

"G-good night."

Dev drew in a deep breath. His heart, his entire being had been sundered and reassembled. Nothing would ever be the same. Yes, he had changed. He loved her more. His love had grown and matured from sapling to oak. His emotions were deeper, more committed. They were entrapped by her for all time. "Good night, Felicity." Dammit, he would give her the space she needed.

Felicity watched him go back down the stairs, then walked on the balcony that overlooked the foyer. "Where are you going?"

"Jogging."

"At this time of night? You could be mugged. You should wear sweats. Where are your running shoes?" She was rattling on, and she knew it. But she was as aroused as he was, for heaven's sake. Did he think he had cornered the market?

He turned at the foot of the stairs to look up at her. "I have things down here, in a room off the kitchen."

"I see."

"I'm sure you do, darling."

His drawling voice hit her gently, like feathery darts. "Be careful."

"I'll be back soon."

"Watch out for . . . everything."

Felicity hated cold showers, but she felt she needed one. So she forced herself to stand under the frigid water, gasping, her teeth chattering.

"I feel the same, but now I have goose bumps," she told her mirror image sourly. She took a hot bath then, washed her hair, cleaned up the bathroom, put the damp towels in the washer, and was tempted to run the vacuum cleaner.

What other job could she do? She needed to be more tired before she climbed into bed.

Was she becoming an insomniac like Dev?

• • •

Dev ran along the quiet streets. The traffic had diminished, but was not entirely gone. Manhattan always had traffic, day or night.

He knew he had a long way to go with Felicity, but he was determined to pursue her until she was his again. It would be a tough road. He saw the changes in her, even as he knew he had changed.

Were Abdul ben Hashallah and Jarred Hamilton only friends to Felicity and his daughter? Or were there deeper feelings there? He knew they had resented his taking charge of Felicity that night. Was it because one or both of the men cared for her?

That would be another obstacle he'd have to overcome.

Dev increased his speed, his breathing coming fast.

Nothing was going to impede the second chance their marriage needed. If in the long run he and Felicity couldn't make it . . .

Dev was now running flat out, his heart pumping hard.

Felicity!

Felicity paced the master suite. Her body still burned for him. Her mind and spirit were in flames.

Too restless to remain in one room, she walked into the smaller bedroom of the suite, where Esther was staying. Dev slept on the other side of the house. She hadn't been over there. She didn't need to venture any further into his aura. His presence was everywhere in the master suite . . . especially in the king-size bed.

Esther turned in her sleep. Felicity leaned down and kissed her, murmuring a Dahrainian rhyme that had never failed to soothe her child. *Their* child! Hers and Dev's. What a miracle that had been, and still was. Everything they'd done together was magic.

She remembered how gleeful Dev had been when she'd told him she'd marry him. He'd been almost childlike.

"Marriage!" he'd exclaimed. "It doesn't seem possible." He'd shaken his head and laughed. When he saw her stiffen, he pulled her into his arms. "Darling, don't draw away. I'm thinking of my friends, Con and Pace. I've always told them I'd never marry, that they would be the ones to carry on with wives and children and I would remain single. Now I'm the first to marry." He kissed her. "I can't wait."

Though he'd sketched his younger years rather thinly, Felicity had known he was an orphan who had been bounced from foster home to foster home until he'd gone to live with a Professor Abrams and his wife. He had loved and revered his adoptive parents—for they had adopted him when he was eighteen—and had grieved when they'd been killed in a car accident a few months after he and Felicity had married.

The Abramses had channeled Dev's boundless

energy into sports and education. He told Felicity how delighted they'd been when he rowed against Oxford, representing Princeton; how they celebrated when he received a fellowship to study in Europe after his graduation. And they'd been thrilled when he told them he was getting married.

Felicity inhaled sharply. Dev was filling the spaces in her life once more, just as he'd done all those years ago.

She straightened and looked around the bedroom that was obviously for a child. Pacer had told her Dev had decorated it for Heller and Con's children. There were masses of dolls and stuffed animals on a window seat. Games were set up on a child-size table. Books lined the walls in chintz-edged bookcases.

Felicity hadn't been surprised that Esther had loved the room on sight. Her rooms in the palace in Dahrain had been much more formal, and though she had been catered to by the household staff, the atmosphere had not been child-oriented. She had claimed the stuffed animals on the window seat at once, putting her own special bear in the place of honor.

Felicity was happy Esther was less aloof with Dev every day, and she often asked where he was and when he would be coming home.

Felicity left the small bedroom and returned to hers. She walked right through it to the sitting room. Sleep was out of the question. Her body still tingled for Dev.

The sitting room was pleasant and restful, with

a fireplace and floor-to-ceiling bookcases. Five daily papers were on the coffee table, three in English, one in German, and one in French.

The day she and Esther moved into the brownstone she had wandered into this room. Pacer had followed her.

"Didn't mean to startle you, darlin'," Pacer had said when she'd heard him behind and whirled, gasping in surprise.

"You could always move like a cat, Pacer Creekwood Dillon."

His smile faded as he looked around the room. "When he first returned from Beirut, Dev wouldn't come out of here for days. He was drunk much of the time."

"Dev drunk? He never drank much."

"He drank a lot when he got back, darlin'. At first he was no better than a sot, drinking continually and fighting Con and me at every turn. Now he's hardened, smooth as a marble. He stays on his feet, but he manages to knock back a great deal of liquor in the twenty or so hours he's up each day."

"Quite a nightlife," she said weakly.

"Can't sleep. Dev's a true insomniac. He goes to the theater or out to dinner, and stays at a favorite restaurant until closing. Most nights he finishes at Pierrot's because it never closes."

She nodded. "I know. Last Friday night, the night before I saw Dev at the theater, Jarred and Abdul took me there." She smiled. "I don't think Abdul approved, but it was very diverting. I had the oddest feeling that evening that Dev was in the area. . . ."

"Your skin itched, did it?"

She drew in a long, shaky breath. "Yes."

Pacer smiled at the irritation in her look. "It always did that when he was around and we used to laugh about it. Remember, Felicity?"

"I remember, but that doesn't mean my skin was itching that night because Dev was around. It's been a while since he and I were together."

Pacer shook his head. "Some things don't change, darlin'. No doubt he *was* around then. Was it after one o'clock in the morning?"

"I don't think so."

He shrugged. "Well, it still could have been Dev." He looked away from her. "He doesn't go to bed until the sun rises."

"And never alone," she said wryly.

"You were dead, darlin'."

"So I was." It stunned her how much it hurt to imagine Dev with other women.

Felicity sank down onto the leather couch. Marrying Haaji some months after he'd taken her to Dahrain had given her a measure of stability, but she'd never been able to put Dev entirely out of her mind. It had hurt so much to dwell on his death, she had fought every memory of him, yet had never succeeded in eradicating his image. There had been nights when she'd wept silently for the husband she'd loved so much, but she had learned to deal with that.

Felicity leaned back and closed her eyes. Now she was back with Dev, in his house. What would happen between them?

She had no idea why she suddenly shivered.

Four

Dev was uncomfortable and edgy. His jog around the area hadn't released all the tension in him. At this time of night he was usually out on the town, eating, drinking, talking, filling up the hours until the sun rose.

What was he going to do now? It was nearly two. Esther was asleep, and no doubt Felicity was too. He couldn't go out. He didn't want to go out. Being near his child and wife was important, but he felt jumpy as a cat on a hot tin roof.

He damn well wanted his wife! Badly. Pacing up and down the book-lined library, he tried to think of a project he might tackle until dawn. Nothing came to mind. There was no space inside him for anything but Felicity.

His life had turned around. There was light and joy in it again, but never before, despite all the pain he'd suffered, had he experienced the terrible uncertainty that was gripping him now. The estrangement between Felicity and himself sparked fresh hurt in him, and not all his rationalizing that it was natural considering their long separation mitigated the sting.

Now that he had them in his house, it should have been easy for him to break down the barriers. Instead, there seemed to be more each day.

Up and down the room he went. When he walked into the side of his desk, he held his knee and cursed roundly.

Felicity wondered if she should go down to the kitchen and make some hot milk. Actually, she didn't like the stuff, but she needed something to help her sleep.

Where was Dev? Had he come back from his run, changed, and gone out for the remainder of the night?

She sat bolt upright in bed. It wasn't her business. Let him go where he chose.

Felicity sighed and sank back. What a mess. She loved the man and he was giving her a headache, indigestion, and insomnia. Damn him.

Dev tried not to think about the bad times. He poured himself some milk and grimaced. He was more used to Irish whiskey before dawn, but no more. The drinking and carousing were out. He was going to spend as much time as possible with his child. There were still some rough moments between them.

A few days ago, when he had offered to take her for her daily walk, she had thrown a tantrum. Pointing to her mother and Pacer, she'd cried, "No, I want to stay with them. If they don't come, I won't go."

Speaking softly but firmly to her, Felicity had taken her daughter from the room. Dev turned to Pacer.

"She liked me. What happened, Pace?"

"Take it easy, chum. These things take time. Remember, your child doesn't know you. She met you for the first time less than a week ago."

"I know, I know. She's confused and bewildered." He stalked across the living room. "Will she ever want to be close to me?"

"Yes, of course she will. You know she's been better with you each day. Felicity said she asks for you when you're not here. Take your time. There are going to be setbacks."

"Right. I realize she's gone through a trauma, coming to a strange country, finding out I'm her father."

His mouth was dry with fear. What if she never loved him? He'd rarely experienced such pain as when she rejected him. He had assumed all the pain in the world had been his when he lost his wife and child, and that he was inured to further punishment. Not so!

Dev scowled and swallowed the last of the milk.

Dawn was a long way off. Maybe he should relax in the hot tub. But the hot tub was in the master suite . . . where Felicity was.

Felicity! He could conjure her up right in front of him, that beautiful face that could tighten with displeasure. Felicity, whom he couldn't seem to reach.

When they'd first been together, she had occasionally seemed remote to him. After a while, though, she'd opened up completely. Now . . . they were two different people!

He sensed a recklessness in her, a fatalistic mystique that was new to him. She was even more exciting than she'd been when they were first married. Tougher, more determined . . . more beautiful.

What had Dev said about a hot tub? Felicity mused. It was time to put thinking on hold. Relaxing was essential. Her insides had turned to jelly. Her being still hungered for Dev.

She wandered around the massive bedroom, touching the elegant rosewood furniture that dotted the room. Hazily, she realized the great worth of the various pieces, and the care with which they'd been bought.

When had Dev changed from a casual observer to collector? When they'd been together, she had been the avid gatherer of art and furnishings. So many times he'd laughed at her when she dragged him to yet another flea market in the Middle East. She'd bought so many lovely things, most of which she assumed had been destroyed.

She sucked in a ragged breath when she spotted the wall rug. She and Dev had purchased it in Lebanon. How had it survived?

She remembered screaming with fear as she and Esther huddled in an abandoned building until the bombing stopped. She figured their apartment building had been destroyed, but she'd never made it back there to find out for sure.

Shaking her head to push the cobwebby memories away, she strode into the small room that housed the sauna and hot tub.

With a sigh she stripped off her nightgown and robe, then hung them behind the door. They had become like lead weights on her skin. Naked she peered down into the swirling water. She felt a momentary guilt at depriving Dev of this luxury. Then she put that aside. The thought of luxuriating in the hot, whirling water was heavenly.

Dev paced his smaller bedroom. It was spacious and comfortable, but it didn't have a hot tub. What he really needed was a good rubdown and a soak, but he discarded the thought of contacting Max at such an hour. He would use his hot tub, and there was a hall entrance to the room, so he wouldn't disturb Felicity.

He was through the door and into the steamy

room before he noticed the music and tub were on. He would have to talk to Mrs. Aldebrand. It wasn't good to keep the tub running at all times, though he noticed the dimly lit room hadn't steamed up completely. The tub couldn't have been turned on to full power.

He flipped on the light and crossed the tiled floor to the tub. His actions were automatic and familiar. He spent long periods of time in the tub to soothe his mind and spirit. Generally he brought a book with him to keep his mind occupied, but he was empty-handed tonight. It would be best to relax, even to snooze, to forget for a while that his own daughter and wife were almost strangers to him. That was a sour acceptance.

He walked to the lip of the tub. This was the very thing to take some of the tension away.

"Hey! What are you doing?"

Felicity had been half asleep, the roiling hot water soothing her. What had woken her, she couldn't say, but when she'd first seen Dev she had been too taken aback to say anything. It hadn't been until he'd stepped to the edge that she'd reacted.

"Felicity!"

Dev had one foot on the top step of the huge tub, the other in the air. The sudden sight of Felicity jarred him and he slipped. He fought to gain his balance and lost.

"Damn!"

With a resounding splash he fell into the water, awkwardly, trying not to hit Felicity. He banged his ankle on the edge of the tub, and his temper flashed. "What the bloody hell . . . ?" he spluttered, spitting out water and swiping the hair back from his forehead.

Her tinkling laugh went through him like a scimitar slicing through soft cheese.

"Dammit, Felicity, what are you doing in here?"

"What are *you*? I thought this was my suite."

"It is, but I thought you were asleep."

"I wasn't, so I decided to use the hot tub. You're the interloper." She flat-handed water at him, catching him in the face, then laughed delightedly.

In the pinkish light cast by the overhead lamp, he could just discern her intriguing silhouette. "You want to play?"

"No! Now, Dev, cut it out." Felicity had no trouble interpreting the feral smile on his face. That look had often been a prelude to ecstasy. Warily she began inching upward. When her foot was caught and yanked, she let out a yelp.

"I like to play," he said silkily, and pulled her under the swirling water, ducking his head as well. Drawing her closer, he wrapped his arms around her and blew air into her mouth, before he let her surface.

"Monster," she gasped, taking a swing at him.

He dodged it easily and caught her around the middle. His hands imprisoning her arms, he swung her up in the air and down next to him. "Take it easy, tiger."

"I'll punch your lights out."

"Still the feistiest female on the planet, aren't you?"

"Yes, and don't you forget it."

"I wasn't the one who forgot, Felicity." His mouth touched her neck in a featherlike caress. "Tell me again what happened to you and Esther."

Her body tensed like an arched bow. "I told you. Actually, it's better forgotten."

"It can't be and won't be by either of us. We need to have it all out in the open." He pulled her closer and gazed down into her eyes. "I want to know about my daughter all those years. I need to know, Felicity. She's my child."

"Yes, she is, and she has the same rock-hard determination."

"Does she?"

Felicity bit back a smile at his pleased tone of voice. "Yes, she doesn't back down easily. Last year, when we were hiding out in the northern part of Dahrain, we stayed in a camp with many refugee children. As it is throughout the Middle East, the boys played all the sports, while the girls sat on the sidelines or worked with their mothers. Not Esther. She made Haaji talk the other mothers into letting their girls play dodge ball with her, and she soon had organized a team to play soccer—her babyish version of it."

Dev laughed. "That would have been something to see."

"I haven't signed her up for a school in Manhattan yet."

"There are a lot of good ones, private mostly. We'll have to apply right away."

Felicity nodded. She was glad for the semidarkness that kept Dev from reading her expression. He was talking about their future, their togetherness. Her heart plummeted and stopped for a moment. Could there really be a future for them? "Ah, I suppose I . . . we could look into that. . . ."

"My country place is in Upstate New York, but we could look in Connecticut or New Jersey, if you think that would be better." Dev struggled to keep his voice neutral.

"Perhaps."

"I know some realty people. I can have them search out a few places and we could look at them."

"Don't you need to be in Manhattan for your work?"

"Yes, but people commute all the time. Will you be going back to work, do you think?" Dammit, they were talking like strangers on a plane, worrying about details and skirting every issue of importance.

"I haven't touched a camera in years, except for some shots of Esther. I wouldn't mind bringing myself into shape professionally, but I wouldn't seek any overseas work again."

"Good."

"But you won't dictate what I do," she said defensively.

"And when did I ever do that?"

"Anytime I let my guard down, Dev. Admit it."

"That's not true. Maybe I overreacted when your safety was involved . . ."

"That's an understatement. You ranted for an hour when you found out I was pregnant."

He scowled. "We were in the Middle East. It was too damned dangerous."

"It wouldn't have mattered where we were." She smiled as she recalled how he'd stormed up and down their small living room, swearing to get her out of the country as soon as he could. But she had talked him into letting her stay.

Dev studied her face, those strong, mobile features, reading her thoughts. "I'm damned if I'll let anyone take you away or hurt you again."

"That's quite a statement from a man who probably feels like killing me himself, now and then."

"That's different," he said gruffly. Her satiny thigh bumped against him, and his libido jumped into high gear. "We have a great deal of ground to cover. Tell me about you and Haaji."

Felicity swallowed. His leg had just touched hers, setting fire to her. "He was devoted to me and to Esther from the start. He was unfailingly kind and generous. He respected my independence and gave me every leeway to expand myself. There was much about his work he discussed with me, and he opened many avenues for me so I could help his people." She shrugged. "He was a good man, brave and caring."

Dev knew by the many articles he'd read about

Haaji in the past week that what she said was true. But it was a jab in his gut to know that any man had been intimate with his wife. He fought down the anger and pain with an effort.

Felicity took a deep breath. "As I told you, I was ill at first. Haaji took care of both Esther and me, got us out of Beirut and to Dahrain.

"About a year later, the parliamentary government he'd helped establish was overthrown by religious radicals. As a result, Haaji was in grave danger everywhere." She drew in a shaky breath. "They killed him shortly after King Ahmed, Haaji's nephew, took power again."

"Go on." Dev stroked her wet hair, his fingers lingering in the strands that clung to her shoulders.

"Dahrain is a beautiful country. Often we stayed in the desert area so Haaji could confer with the tribal sheikhs. Esther was cosseted by the women. They couldn't fathom the light-skinned child with the dark, dark hair."

"Her skin is even lighter than yours." Dev pressed his mouth to her forehead.

"She has my mother's complexion," Felicity murmured, feeling his legs slide under hers.

"I remember. Your mother was very dear to me. It hurt to lose her."

Felicity felt a stab of pain. "Yes, I know. Mother was special. She certainly liked you."

"Yeah." Dev smiled when she laughed. Then he leaned down and kissed her.

Out of breath and dizzy, she pulled back. "I thought you wanted to hear this."

"I do."

"Dev . . . haven't we lost too much?"

"We can find it again."

She faced him. "But you hate me," she blurted out.

"No! Did you think I was dead?"

She swallowed. "I was sure of it. There were too many confirming reports. You were not exactly unknown, and I would never have thought the picture of another man could have been identified as you."

"He nodded. "It was an insane time." But he had been so happy with her.

"Madness." Yet there had been so much joy with Dev.

"Yes."

Silence weighed between them like a millstone.

Unconsciously they'd moved apart. Though their toes still touched, they were aloof from each other. The barriers had re-formed between them.

"Will you answer a question for me?" she asked.

"If I can."

"Why aren't you back there, in Iran, or some other place like Central America where there's fighting? That was lifeblood for you. You thrived on it. Not much came between you and your job, and you were brilliant at it."

"I changed. People do that."

"So they do. And we're two strangers now, Dev. We may not be compatible. . . ."

"I don't buy that . . . yet."

"You're talking with rocks in your jaw. You used to do that when you were really angry. What set you off this time?"

"Maybe you trying to turn what we had into garbage. I revered our marriage."

"So did I." Stung, she rounded on him and shoved him, the water sloshing up over the sides of the tub. "I'm turning into a prune. I'm getting out."

"Wait. Don't you think we should give our marriage a try, if not for our sake, then for Esther's?"

"I think according to international law, we're not married."

"Not according to American law, I'll bet."

"We'll have to check."

Dev snatched her back into his arms. His mouth came down on hers even as she opened it to protest.

Felicity braced herself for savagery. Instead, ineffable sweetness rocked her like an avalanche. Protests, anger, rebellion, melted in the rush of feeling that vibrated between them. She felt as if the world had split open beneath her feet. She was losing her balance and falling, falling, falling down into the abyss, the unknown.

Her hands betrayed her, lifting to the wet mat of hair on his chest, clinging there, curling around the short strands.

"Yes, touch me, Felicity." The words were spoken against her mouth, his breath mingling with hers.

Against her will, her fingers fluttered like moth wings over his body. Was anything more needed to show her parting from this man again would be agony? She had lost him once. Could she stand to go through it a second time if things didn't go well?

Pushing back from him, she surged upward, desperation giving her impetus. She stepped out of the tub, grabbed a towel, and strode from the steamy room.

"Hey! Dammit, Felicity, wait!"

She slammed the bedroom door and leaned against it, her fist shoved into her mouth to muffle the sobs that threatened to burst from her. When she felt him shove against the door, she had to swallow twice to clear her throat. "I thought you said this was my suite."

There was a long silence, then he said, "It is."

She heard him walking away.

Shaking, she made her way to the bed and sat down, still wrapped in the damp fluffy towel. After what seemed like aeons, she stripped off the sodden towel and tossed it toward the chair. It missed.

The past mushroomed over her like a threatening cloud. Her hands shook as she pushed back her heavy, wet hair. Dev! If only things had been different. If only there wasn't uncertainty. If only they could be together . . . Pressing her fingertips against her forehead, she tried to tamp down her errant thoughts.

Too tired to get a nightgown, she crawled between the sheets naked. Funny, she hadn't done that since she'd lived with Dev. She shivered with a remnant of the hot feeling that had swamped her when he'd held her.

She curled into the fetal position, trying to find security. She needed to sleep; she had to sleep! Thinking hurt too much. At last sleep came and brushed away all but the blackness.

Dev was a light sleeper. The years in Vietnam had taught him to be wary. When he opened his eyes, he was instantly alert yet immobile, certain he was not alone in the room. Straining to see in the darkness, only lightly crisscrossed with fading moonlight, he heard breathing. Tightening his muscles, he prepared to move quickly.

When he saw a shadow move away from the doorway, he slid to the far side of the bed and slipped one foot out. His blood went cold as he imagined this person invading Felicity's bedroom, or Esther's. It didn't matter if he was hurt. The intruder would be stopped.

On the floor now on all fours, he crept stealthily around the bed so he would be on the intruder's flank. He prepared to spring just as the person walked through the bars of moonlight inching through the vertical blinds. Felicity!

Heart pounding, Dev rose to his feet in one lithe move. "I can't tell you how glad I am to see you, darling," he whispered. Then he drew in a deep, shuddering breath when she didn't pause on her way to the bed.

Walking around her, he gazed at her face. Her lips were parted slightly, her eyes open wide, but Felicity was asleep.

Dev knew sleepwalking could be caused by a number of things, including stress.

He took her flaccid hand and turned her around, leading her back to the master bedroom. He could feel the coldness of her naked body. Despite his deep concern for her, his libido leaped out of control at the sight of that slender body silvered by moonlight, the long legs tapering to slim ankles and narrow feet.

Felicity had always been beautiful and delicately made. His swarthy six-foot-three-inch body seemed too large and rugged in contrast. Gazing at her still-narrow waist, the upthrust breasts that teased him, he realized that, for him, there was no woman more beautiful than she, nor would there ever be.

"Come on, Felicity, lie down, right here." Getting her into bed wasn't difficult. She seemed amenable to his suggestions, though the fluttering of her eyelids indicated some agitation.

Then she wouldn't release his hand. No amount of gentle tugging or prying worked. He could waken her. No, that wasn't smart. How would she feel? They were both naked. She would be upset, no doubt about it.

So, he climbed in beside her. There would be no problems, he told himself. He would stay well away from her in the king-size bed.

He had to stifle a groan when she curled into him, her hands slipping around his waist as naturally as they always had, the way they used to do when they'd slept together. "I can't stand this," he muttered.

Felicity groaned, her nails digging into him, and he closed his eyes. Perspiration dotted his upper lip; his body trembled.

Felicity whimpered, her hand sliding down over his stomach.

Sinking his teeth hard into his lower lip he willed, with no success, that his body turn off, shut down, desist.

When she touched his arousal, he groaned, his body reacting to her as it always had. "I should kill her for doing this to me. But I love it." His arms tightened around her and he murmured gently to her until she stilled, her hand sliding away from his body.

Not since boyhood had he felt so out of control of his own libido. He had no hope of going to sleep again, nor did he intend to release her.

As he lay there looking up at the ceiling with its crisscrossed pattern of moonlight, a strange contentment crept over him. Not for years had he been in bed as early as he had this past week. Night was not for sleeping. Night brought its own smothering pain, and he would mask it in brassy nightlife. He did everything he could to avoid being alone in his bedroom, yet he never brought women to it. He used a small, exclusive hotel in Manhattan for his ladies. The management was discreet, and he could try to lose himself in sensuality during the dark hours. But not even the beautiful, exciting women who were his companions in the darkness were able to dispel the memories. Memories of Felicity. They intruded every time. It was as though she had emasculated him from the grave. But she hadn't been dead! She had been alive and well . . . and married.

Dev shut his eyes to blank his mind, but he couldn't wipe away the past. He had become a creature of the night, avoiding the sun as an owl or bat would. His lovemaking attempts had been strivings to buttress himself against the long agonizing moments when Esther and Felicity were specters in his brain.

Somehow it had been a solace to come home as the sun was rising, to see the market trucks go by, the morning newspapers dropped at the kiosks. Bits of paper, last night's trash, flew about to catch on a building or flutter in the streets in that early gray hour of morning. To Dev this was the friendliest time of day. There was light, sound, distraction, life, but all was muted, not yet fully awake. He could deal with that, breathe in it.

The morning people had smiles. They didn't move furtively, didn't become ghosts of the past. Daytime was real and he could sleep then, without the banshees.

Still, there were times when he felt threatened even by the day, its normalcy, its upbeat pace, and he would hole up in his study when the sun shone too. It was a blessing to be able to work at home. He was angry and bad-tempered with people a good share of the time.

The night gave him a semblance of living.

Daylight brought a measure of comfort.

Now he was in bed in his own house, after midnight, not after dawn, and the night was amiable, not threatening. Before, when he was caught at home at night, he'd open the windows so the cacophonous traffic sounds would drown out the voices from the past. Tonight the traffic was like an orchestra playing soothing background music to his contentment.

Felicity moved against him. Was she wakening?

When her fluttering fingers closed around his arousal once more, he groaned out loud. Not again! He was just starting to deal with the discomfort. He was going to be in an embarrassing situation if he didn't control—God! She was caressing him, the same way she had when they'd been together. So often they woke to lovemaking, hungering for each other.

Her teasing fingers were a searing recollection, setting him on fire. His reaction surged through him, his blood flooding to the touch of her as he hardened to an impossible degree.

With an explosion he lost all control, his body jerking with passion.

His hand trembling, he grabbed a pillow to wipe her hand and himself. Damn! he thought. Not since adolescence had a woman's touch done that to him. It was humiliating. Moving gingerly, he freed himself from her and sprinted for the bathroom. He grabbed a soft towel and facecloth, then returned to wash and dry Felicity's arm. She didn't move.

Gazing down at her, Dev smiled ruefully. "You still have that almighty power, lady. Dammit, we should have been together on that." He reached out to her, then pulled his hand back slowly. Touching her could set off another chain reaction. He didn't need that! And he sure didn't want to waken her. He frowned. She was sleeping so deeply.

He went back to the bathroom. Maybe after a good brisk shower he would be tired. He could return to the smaller bedroom and fall asleep . . . and hope she wouldn't invade his dreams. Amused irritation filled him. He was like an unfledged boy with her.

When he returned to the bedroom, Felicity was thrashing about. He couldn't leave her like that. He slipped into bed and took hold of her, crooning softly. "I'm here, darling; go to sleep."

"Not tired." Her eyes were still closed, her smile dreamy and soft. Then her eyelids lifted slowly.

Dev braced himself for anger. Instead he got a hot, sensual grin. "Felicity?"

"Make love to me, fool." Her hand slid heavily over his shoulder.

"What?" Her sultry voice was like a caress, enthralling him, rekindling his passion for her. "Felicity?"

"I usually don't have to ask twice. Not that I

mind initiating it, Dev, my love. I don't. After all, we're pretty good at this."

"Are we?"

"You know we are," she whispered dreamily.

He turned on the light above them, making her blink.

"What did you do that for, Dev? Turn it off."

"Just wanted to make sure you knew who it was," he muttered.

"I was expecting Paul Newman, but you'll do." She giggled.

"Thank you." He kissed her fiercely, and her instant response sent him over the edge again. Once more his body surged with passion and he clutched her to him. "Felicity . . . ?"

"Dev, are you being coy? I want to make love. I'm feeling sexy, aren't you?"

"Very."

"Good. Let's talk later then."

Her smile was irresistible, her voice like yards of satin slithering over his skin. He was on fire for her. "This is Dev, darling," he murmured to her, still uncertain she was fully awake.

"I know that." Her dreamy laughter rippled over him, and he kissed her throat.

He held her closer, letting the cascade of sexuality overwhelm him. "You are all of love to me, Felicity."

"Dev, Dev, it's so wonderful." She clung to him, gasping when he entered her swiftly, gently. She began a sensual rhythm, and he drew in his breath sharply.

"Darling! Don't! It'll be too fast."

"I need you . . . now." With a strength born of love, she encased him, held him, sighing with joy as he groaned and gave in.

As one, they loved each other, imitating each other's motions and caresses until they flew apart, swirling in a kaleidoscope of ecstasy. They held each other through the throbbing aftermath, as though they rode out their emotion on a raft tumbling in the ocean.

Felicity yawned and smiled at the same time. "How can we be so incredible . . . over and over again?"

"Don't ask me anything so profound right now. I'm reeling," Dev said into her hair. He tightened his hold when she laughed. It had been great for her too, he thought with relief. The magic was back between them. "Your breasts rub against me so delightfully when you laugh," he murmured. "Have pity, lady. I think I might be in the obituary column if I try any more."

"Poor baby." She kissed his throat. "Have to sleep," she mumbled, then was out like a light.

"Wow, even for you that's fast." Something about this lovemaking bothered him and he needed answers, but at the moment Morpheus beckoned him as well.

Not in years had he been able to drop off to a deep, dreamless sleep so quickly.

He woke only a few hours later, just before the sun rose. A tinge of pinkish gray lightened the sky, and the damp fresh air poured through the open window. For long moments he stared at the ceiling. It hadn't been a dream! He looked down at Felicity, still cuddled in his arms. It hadn't been a wondrous fantasy. She was here with him.

Kissing her on the forehead, he sighed. He had a business meeting with Con and Pacer. If it weren't so important, he'd cancel it.

"You need the sleep, Felicity," he murmured, slipping free of her.

Standing next to the bed, he stared down at her. Had the world righted itself on its axis? Was she really back with him? It seemed too good to be true.

Whistling while laving himself with soap, he pictured the future. A house in the country . . . It would have to be in an excellent school district. His daughter was obviously intelligent and would thrive in an environment where scholastic achievement was rewarded. All at once he had an overpowering need to see his daughter, to talk to her.

He dried quickly, swiped at his hair with a towel, then dressed in a sweat suit. Esther would probably still be sleeping, he thought. He opened her door slowly and peeked inside. The light was on and she was seated, Indian fashion, in the center of the bed. Several open books were lying around her. "Hello," she said. "I like to read. This one about the horse I've read. Dad—Haaji bought me a horse, a beautiful white one. Her name is Fatima." Esther's lip trembled. "Mommy said we couldn't bring her with us now. She said maybe we could get her later."

"I'll check into it this morning. I have a house in the country with very good stables."

Esther's eyes rounded and she straightened. "Do you really?"

"Yes. If we can't get Fatima, perhaps you could choose a horse from our own stables that you like."

"Ye-es, I could do that, but I would still like Fatima."

"I'll do my best."

"Thank you. Are we going to have breakfast now?"

"If you like, you can eat with me, but I think we'll let Mommy sleep. It's very early and she seems very tired."

Esther nodded sagely. "She dreams bad dreams. She used to cry at night sometimes, but then she could never remember what made her cry."

"Maybe if she can get enough rest, the nightmares won't come back."

Esther nodded again. "Shall I get dressed? I know how, but Nanny liked to do it. I can bathe and wash my hair too."

"Good girl. Come down to the breakfast room when you're ready."

He left the room, smiling as he remembered the first morning Felicity and Esther had been there. He'd given Esther directions to the breakfast room. She had listened gravely, then assured him she could find it. "Our palace," she'd explained, "was much bigger than this."

He ambled back to the master bedroom. He

might as well get the clothes he would need that day, then dress in the smaller bedroom so he wouldn't disturb Felicity.

He pushed open the door and stared at the bed for an instant, the outline of Felicity's body drawing his eyes. Then he quietly started across the room.

"What are you doing here?"

He whirled to face Felicity. She was sitting up, the sheet drawn up to her chin. "Darling, I—"

"You promised last night you wouldn't come into this room and already you've broken your word."

"What?" He stared at her, anger filling him. "What the hell is going on here?"

"I think that is just what I asked you." She glared back.

"Felicity! Dammit, what kind of game are you playing? Last night—"

"You promised you would not enter this suite. Now here you are."

His teeth came together with a crack and he strode toward the bed. "We need to talk."

She stiffened and put out one hand. "We'll talk when I'm dressed. Now leave."

He stopped, his eyes narrowing as he studied her face. "You had a nightmare last night."

"I did?" The stiffness drained from her. "I'm sorry if you were disturbed. But they are getting better . . . I think."

His fists slowly opened. "What was it about?"

"I never remember them. Are you going to leave now?"

"You don't recall anything about . . . last night?"

"I never remember. What are you getting at, Dev?"

"Nothing. Esther wants her breakfast. I'll see you later. We do need to talk, Felicity. Understand that." He strode to the closet and pulled clothes from it helter-skelter.

"Dev, wait. I know something's up. What is it?"

"That's what we'll talk about, Felicity, but I think I need to calm down first." He left the room, slamming the door behind him. Could she really have not known they were making love? How could that be? It had seemed so right, so natural. She had been dreamy and casual, but not strange. Damn! He felt trapped in a cobweb.

Questions swirled around his brain as he finished dressing and hurried down the stairs to the breakfast room.

Esther was listening carefully as Mrs. Aldebrand outlined all the things that could be prepared for breakfast. "I think I should like some cereal with fruit, please, and I like toast and jelly."

Smiling at his daughter's British-accented English, Dev strode into the room. "I'll have the same," he said.

"Cereal?" Mrs. Aldebrand asked, her brows rising in disbelief. "Fruit? You never eat breakfast."

"Today I am."

"Very well, sir. Coffee, hot chocolate, and juice are on the sideboard."

"Thanks."

Dev poured hot chocolate and orange juice for Esther and juice and coffee for himself. "Perhaps you'd like to see more of New York today. It's going to be warm and sunny."

"Will I be able to go to the zoo? We didn't have a zoo in Dahrain, but I saw pictures of them."

Dev sucked in a deep breath. Here was a new experience he could share with his daughter. "There's a very good zoo here."

"We didn't have many tall buildings in Dahrain. I like the buildings here, but I like the desert too."

"The desert is beautiful."

Her eyes widened. "Have you been there?"

He nodded. When she beamed at him, he felt as though someone had pulled the chair out from under him.

Five

"We didn't make love!"

Irritation warred with pity and frustration as
Dev faced Felicity that evening after Esther had
gone to bed. It had been a tiring but happy day
for the child. Dev and Felicity had taken her and
the Wendel children to the zoo, and they'd seen it
all.

"Yes, we did," he said softly, aching for her
when her face paled in shock.

"Why don't I remember?" she murmured.

"When did the nightmares start?"

"Not right away, actually." She drew in a shuddering breath. "After I got well, we had a fairly
serene time. Then King Ahmed was deposed and
things changed. Our lives were threatened and
endangered daily. I guess I really didn't realize
how badly it was affecting me until the night-

America's most popular, most compelling romance novels...

Here, at last...love stories that really involve you! Fresh, finely crafted novels with story lines so believable you'll feel you're actually living them! Characters you can relate to...exciting places to visit...unexpected plot twists...all in all, exciting romances that satisfy your mind and delight your heart.

EXAMINE 6 LOVESWEPT NOVELS FOR

15 Days FREE!

To introduce you to this fabulous service, you'll get six brand-new Loveswept releases not yet in the bookstores. These six exciting new titles are yours to examine for 15 days without obligation to buy. Keep them if you wish for just $12.50 plus postage and handling and any applicable sales tax. Offer available in U.S.A. only.

Get one full-length Loveswept FREE every month!
Now you can be sure you'll never, ever miss a single
Loveswept title by enrolling in our special reader's home
delivery service. A service that will bring you all six new
Loveswept romances each month for the price of five—and
deliver them to you before they appear in the bookstores!

Examine 6 Loveswept Novels for

15 days FREE!

(SEE OTHER SIDE FOR DETAILS)

mares started." Her gaze slid away from his. "I thought they were over."

He touched her arm, grimacing when she flinched. "You have my word that I will protect you, that nothing and no one, including me, will threaten you or make you uncomfortable ever again."

"Thank you." Oh, Dev! she thought. Did he know how much she longed to be in his arms? How much she wanted to recall the moment when he had loved her?

"Why don't we go to the mountains? You'll like it there."

"I'm sure I will." Were they strangers again? she wondered sadly. Would they ever behave naturally with each other?

Several days later Felicity was riding a magnificent bay gelding across Dev's estate in the Catskills. Despite the glorious scenery, her mind was filled with thoughts of Dev. Since the evening he'd told her they had made love, they seemed to be living on alien planets. That Dev was unfailingly gentle with her, she had ample evidence. That he was stiff and uncomfortable, she had no doubt. Sometimes she felt like shaking him. She wanted to be closer to him; she wanted to talk. Yet since that night she couldn't remember, he had been different. Always kind to her, but distant.

Their marriage had been a close one, despite their volatile temperaments. The passion between them had always melted anger. When she recalled their times together, she felt as if fire and ice were racing through her veins. They'd taken it for granted, assuming all people had the same wonder of love and passion. How foolish.

Now they faced each other again, not as husband and wife, but as two people from different cultures. Perhaps if the sleepwalking incident hadn't happened, they could have begun to build a new life, but it was there like a wall between them. Was it any wonder feelings were rubbed raw by casual comments?

Felicity urged her horse into a gallop. Were there answers to their predicament?

At that moment, Dev was a spring wound too tight, a blue flame, hot and barely contained. Maybe others wouldn't notice him seething, but she did. And she was doing a little simmering of her own. Where the hell did he get off giving her those heavy looks day and night? If they'd stayed in Manhattan, at least she would have had other people around to cut the tension. That didn't happen here with just the three of them and the servants.

Dev's predilection to withdraw had been one of the things that precipitated arguments when they were married. He would pull a figurative cloak around his feelings, shutting her out as he planned his work strategy, his life. He had tried to change that facet of his personality, but now he was doing it again. And yet he was so gentle with her, seeing to her every wish. Such a paradox. Should she kiss him or kill him?

Felicity slowed her horse and brought it to a stop near a stream, letting it drink as she looked around her. What a view! The mountains were wonderful. She had almost forgotten how lovely Upstate New York was. The mountains had never seemed so tall. The wet autumn weather had cast the multitude of trees into vibrant oranges, russets, golds, and reds, all against an evergreen background. No master painter could have wrought such a mural. This was home!

It was so peaceful. Here in the crisp mountain air with only the whir of eagles' wings and the strident cry of crows to mar the stillness, it was hard to think of the violence and fury she had witnessed in Dahrain. Who could really imagine being threatened by war in such a stunningly beautiful place as this?

Thinking of Dahrain, Felicity knew she could never entirely leave the past behind. She cared too much about the people there. Haaji had encouraged her participation in his world. She had grown close to the shy, gracious desert people who had welcomed her, emphasizing her sameness to them and not the differences. It hadn't been difficult for her to adopt the name of Farisa.

Haaji had taught her to face her dangers. Dev, too, had always understood that she had to be her own woman, though he was inclined at times to want to keep her under wraps.

Felicity sighed and glanced at her watch. It was time to start back. Esther's morning tutoring session would be over soon. She and Dev had decided that until she could be enrolled in a regular school, Esther should be tutored. The young man they'd hired was a university student eager to make some extra money.

Felicity had to laugh when she recalled how Dev had had Con run a check on the young man's credentials. Peter Marshall was working on his doctorate in literature and was glad for the substantial fee Dev paid him to instruct his daughter.

Felicity smiled as she thought of how much Esther loved Dev's country home. And of how fond Esther was of Dev already. Her darling daughter's happiness was no small thing to Felicity. Separating Esther from her father would be so wrong . . . for all of them.

Denying she loved Dev was foolish. Each time he was near her, her pulse fluttered like a schoolgirl's, her stomach flipped, and her body was hot and cold at the same time. Nothing had changed really. Neither space nor time could stem the torrent of feeling Dev had been able to rouse in her almost from the moment they'd met.

A movement to her left told Felicity that the man who'd accompanied her was still there. Dev wouldn't let her ride alone. He said it was too easy to get lost in the area.

Where was Dev at that moment? she wondered. He'd told her he had to see Con and Pacer about business that morning. The Wendels were spending a week at their own country home, a few miles from Dev's place. Their eldest son, Simeon, had

stayed in New York City with their housekeeper,
since he had to go to school, but Heller and Con
had brought the twins with them. Was Dev still at
The Wendelses' ? She wanted to see him, but she
wished him on the moon too. Dear Lord, what a
tangle!

"Dev, stop that damned pacing." Con glared at
his friend. "Nothing will be accomplished if you
keep galloping up and down the room like a
gorilla."

Dev scowled. "This damned house is too big. No
one needs a library this large." Dev had always
loved the Wendel country home, but Felicity and
Esther were at his house. He should be with them.
The beautiful book-lined room caged him.

"The man is upset," Pacer drawled. "Else he
wouldn't be blaming you for livin', Con." Pacer
beamed when Dev shook a fist at him. "We haven't
gone a few rounds in a long time, chum. Like to
try?"

"You broke my nose when we were in Saigon."

"You were lucky that was all that was broken.
Deciding to punch out an entire bar filled with
soldiers wasn't a good idea."

"They were going to rape that little girl."

"You should have waited for backup. Con was
coming to meet us with half the unit."

"We beat them, didn't we? Why the hell did you
start on me after we were done?"

"Because of you I got a black eye and broke my

tooth. You needed a little punishing for being so impulsive. I'll be damned if I let you get me into something like that again."

"You know you'll join in anytime he pulls something," Con said. "Can we leave the games until we settle this? Dev, come on, sit down. You're on edge. And quit encouraging him, Pace. You've been up for two nights and you're not at your best."

The door opened and Heller entered, glancing at each one in turn. "I don't mean to interrupt, but . . . is something wrong?"

Con walked over to her and gently kissed her once, then again. "Everything's fine, sweetheart. Dev's just missing Felicity and Esther."

"Let her stay," Dev said. "She's tough and smart." His smile was crooked. "Tougher and smarter than all of us."

Pacer nodded. "Come sit by me, Heller, darlin'."

Heller smiled at them all and took a chair next to Pacer. When she gestured to Dev that he sit on the other side of her, he did so at once.

"She should have been here from the beginning," Pacer said. "It might have calmed the idiot." He nodded toward Dev.

"Very funny."

Heller patted Dev's hand and smiled at him. "Don't pay any attention. When Con thought I was in danger he was nearly out of his mind."

"I remember." Dev smiled at his friend, then the smile faded. "I want to know, Con, why those contacts of yours said to watch your backside if you do business with the Dahrainians."

Heller gasped. "Would there be a connection between this and Felicity?"

Con shook his head. "Not to worry, Heller. I'm sure it's nothing. Besides, both Dev and I have security systems that no one has cracked. We're just mulling things over, checking, hoping we're two jumps ahead of things."

He exhaled heavily. "There have been some strangers spotted in the area. That we know. But we're also pretty sure no one knows Felicity and Esther are here. Pacer was able to get some people who are often used by the government to sweep the area. They'll set up an even more elaborate security system around Dev's house." Con smiled at his wife. "I'm sure there's no problem, but there's no harm in being extra-careful."

Heller nodded. "But how could anyone find out about your place, Dev? You told me that some of your closest friends don't even know about it. Do you really think these strangers are looking for Felicity and Esther?"

Dev touched her hand. "That's what we're going to find out."

"See," Con said, "things are under control."

"Then why do you, Pacer, and Dev look so anxious?"

Felicity turned her horse and began a circuitous route back home. When she came to a flat mountain meadow, she dropped her hands and let the skittish horse have his head.

With the wind tearing at her face and hair, some of the pressures of the past days seemed to be swept away.

Crack!

Instinctively, she dropped low over her horse. That was a gunshot. She'd heard too many sounds like it in Dahrain not to recognize it. She looked behind her and saw Mandell, her guide. He was still in the saddle, but barely hanging on. The horse was slowing, and Mandell waved at her to keep going.

"Are you all right?" she called, galloping back to him.

"Get out of here, ma'am," he said as she pulled up beside him. "Must be hunters. Hurry."

"No, I'm not leaving you."

Crack!

Felicity felt the sting in her arm, and the impact almost knocked her from the saddle. "Ride!" she shouted. "We have to get out of here." She turned her horse toward the distant forest.

"You go, ma'am. Please."

She grabbed Mandell's reins. "We'll go together," she told him grimly. "Can you grasp the pommel? Good; hang on." She wrapped his reins around her saddle horn, leaned over the powerful animal's neck, and dug her heels into her horse's sides.

Responding to the command, the gelding jumped into a gallop, pulling the other horse along. Together they sped over the hilly open ground.

Shots zinged all around Felicity as they raced

for cover. Not once looking back, she could only pray that Mandell was still in the saddle and had not been struck again.

The forest seemed a hundred miles away. She kept her gaze fixed on it and didn't slacken speed.

Dev leaped to his feet. "I'm going." He strode to the door, leaving Heller openmouthed and his friends staring after him thoughtfully.

"Dev! Wait." Heller reached him as he opened the door. "What is it?"

Pacer stood and grabbed his jacket. "He thinks something has happened to Felicity, or maybe Esther. He's usually right when he gets these feelings."

"I don't know which one," Dev said, "but something's wrong. I have to go."

"Take the chopper," Con said.

"I was planning on that." Dev gave them a lop-sided grin, then was gone.

He knew Pacer was behind him, but didn't look back as he hopped into a Jeep. The helipad was on a knoll some distance from the house. He felt the Jeep rock as he slammed it into first and pressed down on the starter.

"Almost didn't make it," Pacer said casually.

"You could have outrun it," Dev said, not looking at his friend as they bounced over the rough ground.

By the time they reached the chopper the rotor

blade had already whirred into life. They bent low as they raced for the open door.

"Your place, Mr. Abrams?" the pilot asked as the helicopter lifted from the ground.

"Yeah." Dev glowered at the pilot.

"He'd rather be flying it himself," Pacer explained. "He was a hell of a chopper man in 'Nam."

"I know." The pilot grinned at Dev's black expression. "Mr. Wendel told me not to let Mr. Abrams near the controls."

"Figures," Dev muttered. He stared out the window, gnawing on his bottom lip.

"Easy. We'll get there."

Dev rounded on his friend. "She's in danger, right now. I can feel it."

"Open up the throttle on this thing, will you?" Pacer said to the pilot, who glanced at him and nodded.

In no time they were circling Dev's hideaway, then the machine glided down to a soft landing.

Dev and Pacer were out the door instantly, running toward the Jeep parked there.

Dev flung himself behind the wheel and fired the engine. The Jeep roared down the road.

"How the hell can anyone find her here?" Pacer asked.

"I don't know, Pace, but I will find out. If anything has happened to her or Esther . . ."

Pacer squeezed his shoulder. "It hasn't."

Neither man said any more as they sped down the narrow twisting lane. Dev screeched the Jeep to a stop in front of the house. Peter Marshall was

BLUE FLAME • 103

standing on the front porch, rifle to his shoulder, aiming at them.

Seeing who it was, Peter lowered the gun. "Sorry, Mr. Abrams, I didn't know it was—"

"My wife, my daughter?" Dev jumped out of the Jeep and ran up onto the porch.

"Your daughter's inside. The emergency crew was here with a doctor, but—"

Dev pushed past the tutor and ran into the house. "Tell me what happened," Pacer said to Peter.

"Mrs. dai Haaji has been wounded in the shoulder. Mandell, the stable man, is more seriously hurt. They were taken out of here by chopper to the hospital in town. The police have been informed. Esther is fine and in the library with the cook, who, I understand, is a very good shot."

"No doubt." Pacer smiled thinly and strode past him, then paused. "Has security been informed?"

"Yes, sir. Everything is being done. The grounds are being swept now by people with dogs."

"Good. How the hell did anyone find her?"

"I don't know, sir." Peter looked anxiously toward the woods.

Inside the house Pacer heard muffled noises coming from the library and headed that way. He stopped on the threshold. Dev, his face taut with pain, was holding Esther close as he spoke with the cook.

"And when did they leave, Jasper?"

"The State Police helicopter picked them up.

The lieutenant was going to inform you at Mr. Wendel's. Did he?"

"Something like that," Dev muttered, kissing the little girl on the cheek. "It's all right, honey. Mommy is fine."

"She was bleeding." Esther's bottom lip trembled.

"But she was not badly hurt. Would you like to fly in a plane and see her?"

She wiped away her tears. "Could we do that?"

"We'll go at once with Uncle Pacer."

Pacer pushed away from the doorjamb and walked over to them. "That's right. We'll go now and see Mommy."

Within minutes Dev had the journey organized. Once more Con's pilot took them aloft, Esther strapped into the seat beside him, round-eyed and questioning everything.

"I want to know who's behind this," Dev whispered grimly to Pacer.

"The word is out. I called some of my people before we left. They'll throw out the net."

"I won't have her hurt."

Pacer patted his shoulder, then leaned forward to point out a landmark to Esther.

Dev was in hell. It was almost as bad as all those years he'd been without Felicity. She'd been shot at, almost killed. Even as those black thoughts swirled around him, he could still admire the guts it had taken for her to go back for Mandell.

Though the small town of Woodbourne was a mountain community, many of the inhabitants were people from New York who wanted country hideaways—and the best medical care possible. The hospital was up-to-date, and always had enough money to pay its staff and purchase new equipment. It met the most rigid standards of excellence.

Dev knew all this and was thankful for the many times he had coerced his wealthy friends into contributing to the hospital. But would the care be good enough? Did Felicity need more? Picturing his wife in the operating room, he felt bile rise in his throat. Felicity!

The flight took less than fifteen minutes. Since the pilot was able to land on the hospital helipad, they were in the building in no time. They entered through the emergency doors and hurried to the treatment center.

"Mommy!" Esther saw her mother sitting on a gurney and started to run.

"Wait a minute, sweetheart," Pacer whispered to the little girl, sweeping her up into his arms.

Dev kept going, his gaze on Felicity, his heart thudding against his ribs.

"Dev, what are you doing here?" Felicity's mouth fell open as Dev brushed past the attending physician. He caught her in his arms, embracing her warmly, but gently. "Dev?" Automatically, she clasped his neck with one arm to balance herself.

"Ah, sir, excuse me, I need to finish the dressing." The doctor was torn between amusement and irritation.

"What? Oh, yes, continue," Dev said offhandedly, not releasing Felicity. "How badly is she hurt?

Has she had the best care? Does she need special-
ists?"

The doctor stared at him, a small smile flitting
over his face. "If you could stand to one side . . . ?"

Dev moved clear of the doctor, but didn't release
Felicity.

After a few more minutes of work, the doctor
stepped back. "There. It was a crease with little
loss of blood. Your arm might sting for a day or
so, Mrs. dai Haaji, but you should be fine."

"See, Dev. I'm all right."

"I almost lost you . . . again. Dammit, that's not
all right."

The doctor glanced at Dev, obviously startled by
his harsh voice, then turned back to Felicity. "I
would recommend that you stay off your feet for a
day or so, Mrs. dai Haaji. As I said, the wound is
minor, but it wouldn't hurt to rest for a little
while. I foresee no problems if you exercise rea-
sonable care."

"She will," Dev said as Felicity was opening her
mouth to respond.

"Dev." She lifted her hand to his face, tracing
the tight lines from eyes to mouth.

"You'll need a wheelchair," the doctor said, "Hospital policy."

"I'll carry her," Dev said.

The doctor shrugged. "As you say."

"Why do you have to be carried, Mommy?" Esther asked, great interest in her voice. "Are you
hurt a lot?"

"No."

"Yes," Dev answered at the same time. "We're going to take good care of Mommy, aren't we?"

Esther nodded solemnly. "Yes, and I know how to."

"So do I."

"She can have a night-light," Esther said solemnly, looking up at her Uncle Pacer, who smiled and nodded.

Pacer set the girl down and walked over to Felicity. He kissed her gently on the lips, then whispered, "Stop scaring us, lady."

"I'll try. How is Mandell?"

"He's critical, but expected to make it." Pacer smiled when Felicity sighed audibly. "Would we get you anyone who wasn't as tough as Dev, lady?"

"There's nobody as tough as Dev," she said dryly. When she glanced at Dev and saw the slashes of red high on his cheeks, she cocked her head to one side. "Embarrassed or angry?"

"I haven't been anything but angry since I first saw you." He kissed her hard.

"Everybody kisses you, Mommy. Are they supposed to do that all the time?"

Even Dev chuckled. He released Felicity for the first time and leaned down to the child. "Could I kiss you?"

Esther nodded shyly, holding up her cheek.

Dev kissed her, his lips lingering there. "Thank you."

"You could also tell me a story at bedtime," Esther informed him generously.

"Thank you."

"Come with me, Esther," Pacer said, "and we'll see if we can find some ice cream." He took her hand and followed the doctor and nurse from the treatment room.

When Dev was alone with Felicity, he lifted her hand and studied the palm as though he could see the future in it. "I will never let anything or anyone part us, Felicity, even if you never want to be my wife again. And I damn well won't let anyone hurt you, not ever." He sucked in an uneven breath. "They'll pay for this."

"Dev, don't. I'm so tired of vengeance, violence. I don't want it in our lives anymore."

He swallowed and nodded, cupping her hands against his face. "Are you all right?"

"Yes. I was scared at first, but then things got too hectic for fear."

He smiled that twisted smile she loved so much. "You're one tough lady."

"I've had to be."

"You've changed, but parts of you are the same. Courage was woven into your fabric, Felicity. You've always had it."

"I must have learned it from you."

He shook his head, bending close to her. "No. It's been yours since childhood."

Felicity couldn't have stopped leaning up to him if she'd been ordered to do so. "Now, how would you know about that?"

"Easy. I know everything about you." He inched closer.

"Know-it-all." She stretched upward.

"About you I am."

She saw behind his satirical grin. "You've had to be tough too."

"I was in a tough business."

"But you went beyond it to hard, steely." Their lips were almost touching, and she noticed his infinitesimal withdrawal.

"Yes," he said.

"And you can't go back."

"Probably not," His head lowered again and his tongue touched her bottom lip. "Planning on cracking the steel plate?"

"It's a challenge."

"And you always liked challenges." He gently bit her lip.

"Ouch." Felicity closed her eyes, trying to stem the ecstasy that swelled like the tide. It was as though they'd made love yesterday! Her eyes flew open. They had made love a short time ago . . . and she didn't remember. Damn the fates! Damn Deveril Abrams for his power.

"Bite me back, Felicity. Revenge can be sweet."

"I'll hurt you."

"Gnaw away."

"Dev."

"Yes?" His mouth coursed down her neck.

"Stop. We're in a treatment room."

"I know."

"Esther is here."

"I know that too. I brought her."

"I forgot."

"Kiss me."

She turned, and pressed her mouth to his. Blood roared through her. Cascades of passion had her gasping. She had to hold on to his shirtfront to keep from falling. Women didn't faint from emotion anymore. Did they?

"Darling."

Had he said that or had she? Electricity was crackling around them, creating a lethal aura that would smite all but those it enclosed.

Her hands tightened on him. Time enough later to question what was happening, its familiarity. Now she was in some sort of shock. Better to ride it out . . . and enjoy it.

Six

The days following her return from the hospital were both amusing and irritating to Felicity. She told Dev she didn't need to be carried wherever she went, though having him hold her made her very happy. She tried not to dwell on that.

It stunned her that all the wonderful feelings she and Dev had shared had been put on hold. Now their emotions were coming out of hiding with a vengeance.

She only had to look at Dev to become dry-mouthed and wanting. She would have sworn that such feelings, buried for so long, could not resurrect themselves hotter than they'd been. But they had. She wanted him so much, every fiber of her being ached with desire. The sensation that they had made love just moments ago, instead of years, was a mounting irritant. If they didn't soon make love she would . . . she would bash him. It flummoxed her that she couldn't come right out and say that to him. She'd often done that before she'd lost him.

One day after lunch Dev carried her to the pool, setting her down on an overstuffed chaise longue. The autumn sun shone through the Plexiglas ceiling of the room, lending it a steamy southern comfort.

She looked around. "How rich are you?" It pleased her to see him unbend, his tight features relax into a grin. He was no longer the carefree, laughing man she'd married, but sometimes there were glimpses.

"Rich enough to pay the bills," he answered.

"When I think of how broke we were most of the time . . ." She smiled and shook her head. "It seems like another lifetime."

"We were happy," he said abruptly.

When he would have straightened away from her, she caught his chin. "So we were. Don't be so prickly with me."

He kissed her. "I'm trying. Shall I carry you into the pool?"

"Don't be silly. I'll walk down those steps . . . with you."

As they started down the steps, she felt her own old power coming back. The sensation that she and Dev could move mountains had been a constant when they were married. It was seeping into her pores once more.

He slipped his arms around her waist. "You're

too slender, but you still have the sexiest body I've ever seen."

"And you've seen plenty." They were on the last of the broad steps, and she gave him a push. Off balance, he went under. Laughing, she eased herself into the water, loving the silken feel of it on her skin.

When Dev came up directly in front of her, she kissed him. "You're in my way, mister."

"Am I?" he asked huskily. "Do it again."

Once more their lips met, and they sank to the bottom of the pool.

"You're fire to me, lady," Dev told her when they surfaced.

She laughed shakily. "You give off a few sparks yourself."

The rest of the afternoon they stayed close, touching every chance they got. Dev would reach over to show her an article he was reading, his lips feathering her cheek. Felicity would lean against him, his warm, muscular body a sensual comfort.

She felt like screaming that she wanted him to love her, not cosset her, but she said nothing.

The afternoon sped by far too quickly. Words weren't spoken, but need vibrated between them.

That evening, when Felicity was in her bedroom readying herself for dinner, she made the call she hadn't wanted to make. But it was time to deal with an ugly reality.

Abdul ben Hashallah answered the phone on

the second ring, and she quickly told him about the attack. Although Dev hadn't mentioned his suspicions to her, she knew he didn't believe the gunshots had been an accident. She didn't either.

"I know it sounds crazy, Abdul, but do you suppose it could be the rebels who assassinated Haaji?"

"It does not sound crazy at all, madame," Abdul said slowly. "King Ahmed is coming to this country in less than a week. It would be a good opportunity for the rebels to commit another terrorist act, to draw world attention to their cause."

Felicity's grip tightened on the phone. If anything happened to King Ahmed, the future of Dahrain would be bleak indeed. "But what would they want with me?"

"You are the widow of Haaji dai Haaji, a great enemy of the revolutionaries. To kill you and your daughter Suni would bring great pleasure to them."

"Suni?" Felicity whispered, fear paralyzing her limbs. She had hated living in terror in Dahrain, and had been relieved to return at last to the States and leave all of that behind. To have the terror follow her here . . .

"What can we do, Abdul? De—Mr. Abrams has a sophisticated security system here and has posted guards, but we can't stay here forever."

Abdul didn't speak for a long time. At last he said, "I will see what I can find out about the man who attacked you, madame. Perhaps you would be safer at the consulate. . . ."

"Oh, no, Abdul." She couldn't leave Dev again,

even temporarily. "I'm sure I'll be safe here for now. But you will call when you find out anything, won't you?"

"Yes, madame. I will call."

Felicity was surprised that Abdul called her back the next morning. Dev was out riding—in other words, Felicity thought, checking the area for any signs of intruders—so she took the call in his study.

"Yes, Abdul? Have you found out anything?"

"I have, madame. It is as I suspected. Several revolutionaries have entered this country illegally, and I am certain you and the king are their targets. I urge you, madame, to come back to the consulate where we can protect you." He paused. "You are very dear to the Dahrainian people. They would not want anything to happen to you."

Felicity stared blindly across the room, uncertain what to do. Dev could protect her too. He had vowed to do so. And that was dangerous. If he knew for certain her life was threatened, he would take on the assassins single-handedly—and maybe get himself killed in the process. And Esther! She was an innocent child, but if these murderous rebels had the opportunity, they would kill her as well. Perhaps Abdul was right. Perhaps she—and her family—would be safer if she went to the consulate.

"Madame," Abdul said, "I realize you feel protected where you are, but your American friends do not know these people as we do. I am certain we will be able to capture these men by the time the king arrives. Let us protect you. Haaji would want this. So would the king."

"I suppose you're right," she said reluctantly. "But I don't think Mr. Abrams will let me return to New York without him."

"I have already thought of that, madame. If you could drive to the small town, Woodbourne, we could arrange to pick you up there."

"I don't drive alone. I always have a chauffeur."

"Ah. Then I suggest you say you need to shop in the town. Go into one of the stores on the north side of the main street, then leave by the back door. There is an alley behind those stores, and we could pick you up there."

Felicity was impressed by Abdul's knowledge of the town. He had been busy in the last fourteen hours.

"All right," she said. "How about tomorrow, Friday? Mr. Abrams has a meeting with some business associates that will probably last most of the day."

"Tomorrow will be fine, madame. Can you be in town by nine o'clock?"

She stared out the window, watching Dev ride up to the stables, his dark hair gleaming in the sun. Oh, God, how she loved him. "I wonder if he'll ever forgive me for leaving him again."

"What did you say, madame? I didn't quite hear you."

"Nothing, Abdul. I'll be there at nine o'clock."

"Very good, madame. And, madame, this is the best thing."

After his ride, Dev decided to swim. He reveled in the stretching of muscles, the constant massage of the water. It had cost the earth to put in the regulation twenty-five yard pool, but he didn't care. While swimming he could put his problems in the proper slot, and free himself of black thoughts.

He was surprised when he felt a surge of water that signaled someone else had entered the pool. No one usually used it but himself. Figuring it would be Pacer, who was as good a swimmer as he, if not better, he paid no more attention.

He turned at the end of the pool and started back—and was stunned by the feathery caress on his inner thigh. He swallowed water and came up coughing. "What the hell . . . ?"

"Hi." Felicity stared at his gaping mouth and laughed.

"Are you asleep again?" he asked.

"Not a chance."

Her sultry voice had him shaking his head. "Good. Are you going to swim?"

"I thought I might. Would it bother you?"

"Your swimming would not bother me," he said softly.

"What would?" She pressed against him, and her wet body set his on fire.

"Now, that's a very leading question."

"Yes, isn't it," she murmured in his ear.

"Felicity . . . are you all right?" His hands clenched around her waist.

"Ouch! Going to pinch me to death?" Her tongue touched the edge of his ear. "I'm just fine."

"Just making sure . . . you don't get away." He still wasn't convinced she was totally aware of what she was doing, or whom she was with.

"Don't you want me near you?" she asked.

"Very much."

"Well, then." She let her leg slip between his. "I locked the doors."

"All of them?" He was intrigued and captivated by the devil-may-care look in her eyes. Would he ever understand this woman?

She nodded. "What do you think?"

In a surge of passion, he hauled her close to him, keeping them both above water with a strong kick. "Fine with me," he said hoarsely, his lips against hers.

Emotion thrust them both into the whirlpool of love that had always been theirs. The world spun around them in a kaleidoscope of colors, the thrumming of their blood loud in their ears.

Felicity kissed his strong, tanned neck. Her lips found the pulse at its base, and the throbbing in his veins seemed to flow from his body into hers.

He kneaded her breast through her Lycra suit, his thumb sliding over the hard bud at the tip.

Like stones they sank to the depths of the pool.

Out of breath, Dev pushed upward and they surfaced, their unsteady breathing the only sound for a moment. Then Dev moved away, and Felicity felt a stab of uncertainty.

"Dev?"

"I'm just finding us a more comfortable spot. Making love in the water is nice, but I could forget myself in you, Felicity. Drowning is not high on my list of priorities."

"Chicken."

Her laugh was like the purring of a cat. It ran over his skin like a caress. Yet . . . he felt a chill wariness too. Something was not right. A bell was ringing flat. What was discordant, out of sync? Why was there a smell of menace? If he thought about it, he would figure it out . . . but not while Felicity was touching him in such a hot and tender way. She melted his caution, seared his sixth sense. Want overcame prudence, and the nebulous foreboding was pushed away. Time enough to delve into his subconscious alarms later. Right now he needed the closeness his wife was offering him. Still, he held back. "I want to protect you."

"No. I am protected." The lie came easily because she wanted him so much, and hated anything that might possibly be a barrier.

"You are?" Dev was jolted again, his reason piercing his passion.

"Don't stop now. Please!" Her lips pressed to his, open and wanting, and he had no more arguments.

He hoisted her effortlessly onto the tile deck, then swung up beside her. "I think you'll like this."

He smiled down at her and led her to an enclosed area on one side of the pool. It was a private room that no one but he had used until now. After unlocking it with a key he took from a hidden niche, he pushed open the door with the flat of his hand. "What do you think?"

"A seraglio?" She smiled, but there was a touch of vinegar in her voice.

"Not so far. This is for me alone. You're my first houri." He chuckled softly.

She punched his arm, her smile more natural. "It is pretty in here. The plants are exotic but serene. With the view of the mountains, this would be restful, great for reading or studying."

"Or brooding."

"What did you say, Dev?" She had moved farther into the spacious sunroom, and turned to face him.

"What was that you were doing in the water?" Approaching her, he held out his arms.

"Oh. That."

"Yes." He watched her walk back to him slowly, aware that his body was hardening even more and that, in his skimpy bathing suit, his reaction was very visible to her.

She paused only inches away from him, her gaze running over him. "I think I get your drift."

The mirth welling in her eyes had colored them a velvety purple, making his heart thud out of rhythm. Had it been aeons since he'd seen that special softness in her eyes? He reached out his finger and barely touched the nub of her breast.

"You're not quite so obvious, but your emotions show too."

"Rat."

"You were teasing me, sweetheart. Just thought I'd take a shot." He moved closer so his lower body rubbed her abdomen. "Going to keep me dangling?"

"But you're not . . . dangling."

"Brat. Putting me off?"

She swallowed, her laughter dying as she stared up at him. "I should."

He kissed the tip of her nose. "I hope you won't. I need your passion."

"You were always very direct." She stretched upward, her arms clasping him loosely around the neck.

"Ummm, yes." His hands settled at her waist.

When their mouths touched, there was still space between their bodies. But there was lightning and crashing cymbals in the crackling sensations that encircled them.

Felicity made the first move, her hands moving down his chest, twining in the wet dark hair there, tugging sharply. "I want you."

"How convenient. I feel the same way."

"Good."

When he bent and scooped her up into his arms, she laughed. "You used to do that all the time."

"Carry you?" She nodded, and he smiled. "It's still one of my favorite things to do. Holding on to you is the one sure way of knowing you won't disappear on me." When she hid her face in his neck, passion flooded him, along with a shiver of

trepidation. Something just outside his conscious-
ness was trying to signal him.

A foggy dread had him turning to look at the
closed door behind them, as though there were
some threatening specter there. Then, shrugging
off the silliness, he strode to the large daybed,
leaned down, and pushed a button on the bedside
console.

She chuckled. "A bed opens up before your eyes,
sheets and all. It *is* a damned seraglio."

"You could say that." It didn't seem the time to
mention that he'd often slept out here during the
day, finding it easier to close his eyes in a bed
that wasn't really a bed. Beds could be so per-
sonal, such prods to memory. Beds were diaries
of love in three dimensions, and he hadn't needed
that.

It was a Danish-style bed with a thick mattress
and a plain, heavy white oak frame. "No one comes
here but me."

"What a waste."

"Until now, darling." He laid her on the bed and
followed her down. His mouth nuzzled her navel
as he gently pulled off her suit. When she was
nude, he lifted his head to look at her. "I won't let
you build barriers, sweetheart. We are here to love,
not argue."

"So we are." She cupped his face in her hands,
staring at him before pulling him to her and
pressed her mouth against his.

The world tipped, then spun out of control as
they were pulled into a vortex of erotic joy.

Dev let his hands flutter down over her thighs. Her warm skin was like golden silk. Slowly he moved one hand upward until he felt the sudden moistness of her lower body. Pushing the heel of his hand there, he began a smooth rhythm that Felicity was soon following with her entire body.

Her moans were echoed by him. Each breath was pulled from them as though a force reached into the core of them for it. Desire was a flaming meteor.

Felicity flung her head back, as though she were calling for him. He answered. He mated his mouth to hers, his fingers still entwined with the curling hair at her body's joining. As his tongue entered her mouth and danced with hers, his thumb continued the rubbing caress, then his finger found her center and imitated the same wonderful pulse beat.

She arched her back as the heat built in her. Her hands, grasping his head, threatened to yank every hair from its root. "I . . . have . . . always . . . thought . . . you . . . were . . . a . . . a wonderful . . . lover."

Her gasps went through him like spears of heat, firing him as never before. His body bucked as though to control the waterfall of passion engulfing him. He gazed at her and saw his hunger mirrored in her eyes. His hands ran up the backs of her legs, and opened and closed on her buttocks in loving caress.

"Dev!" Her whispered demand had him chuckling huskily.

Settling his body over hers, he nudged her legs apart. It was all so familiar and beautiful, yet all so brand-new. They'd made love a thousand times, but now it was the first, beautiful moment for each.

His tongue lapped gently at a tear that trickled down her cheek. "Crying?"

She nodded. "But not sad."

"You're beautiful, sweetheart."

"You're pretty too." Her throaty laugh jolted through him.

"Remember to laugh like that when I'm inside you."

"You still say the most outrageous things."

He didn't answer. He moved back instead.

"Leaving so soon?"

"You know better." His breath bubbled over her skin as he trailed his mouth down her body.

When his tongue entered in the most intimate caress, her body arched again, her breath expelling from her in a long sigh. "I've needed you so much."

"As I've needed you . . . and thought I'd never have you again."

At last he took her in fierce gentleness, rocking them both. A tidal wave swept over them, tossing them in elemental, sexual fury. They were fused by the storm, owned by it. Shudder after shudder sent tremors through their bodies until they crescendoed together, and each cried out the other's name.

Moisture coated them as they drifted to earth once more.

"Was it ever that good for you before?"

Dev heard the trembling question behind her question. He kissed her chin, then let his mouth settle at her ear and sighed. "Despite what everyone thinks, including Con and Pacer, I am not a sexual athlete, darling. I'll give you more details at another time. There is one thing . . ." He raised up on one elbow so he could look at her. "If I could have buried myself in every woman in the world to forget you, I would have. But each time I was close to a woman, really close, something spoiled it. You were too fresh. I had no doubt that in time I would overcome—Ouch! That hurt."

"Then don't get so graphic with me."

"Was it ever that good for you?" The question ripped him apart to ask.

She touched his face with one finger. "I was Haaji's wife and he was good to me . . . but he'd been emasculated two years before when a bomb went off in his limousine. I would have gladly let him love me, but . . . he couldn't."

Dev leaned down and kissed her mouth. "Have I told you that I think you're very brave?"

"I'm not really, but I learned how to survive. I knew I had to do that to protect Esther."

Minutes drifted by. Had they been together an hour or an age?

"Darling?" Dev rubbed against her.

"Fool, you *are* a sexual athlete." Amusement

colored her voice as she laced her fingers behind his neck. "I feel a need myself."

To Dev's surprise it was speedier than before, hotter. Need had telescoped all their emotions, and passion was theirs.

River after river of feeling bucked her body as she felt his velvet intrusion.

"Dev, Dev . . ."

"Shh, Felicity, darling. I'm loving you."

"I want you so."

He entered her in one smooth stroke, taking her even as she enclosed him.

As one they began the rhythm that cascaded them into an emotional stream so strong, they were tossed and turned as helplessly as a leaf in the tide. As one they came together in an earth-shattering explosion, fused by the fire of love that had grown and swelled in them.

Dev eased off her and lay beside her. He turned to her to say something and saw she was asleep. Concerned, he studied her closely, his gaze and hands going over her in loving care. Was she ill? He didn't recall her ever sleeping so quickly or so deeply.

Would she remember their loving this time? Why had it been a blank the other time?

His mouth was near hers, as though he would inhale her every breath . . . each of which came slowly, pulled from her lungs as though breathing were scarcely necessary in the semicoma she was caught in.

"No matter what you say, my sweet, irritating

wife, you are going to see a doctor. There are too many mysteries about you. We'll start with the inside and work out."

So many things had been off base since her return. He was sure there was much she wasn't telling him. That was going to change. By the time they returned to Manhattan, they would be married again and he would know a great deal more about her.

Sighing his contentment at his plans, he closed his eyes. He was tired to the bone. Sleeping with Felicity in his arms would ensure that he had a long, peaceful nap.

Was it hours or moments they slept? No matter. Their need for each other had not been assuaged. They slept, swam, talked, and made love again. Too soon the interlude was gone.

That evening, Felicity called Abdul to confirm their plans before she went down to dinner. It had been unnerving waking in the sunroom wrapped in Dev's arms. The familiar feelings of safety that had washed over her had brought tears to her eyes. He had cut through all her defenses. He wouldn't be stopped.

It was that knowledge that hardened her resolve to leave him. He would tackle the terrorists like a bull on the charge, and they would kill him. She had to act.

She knew she had to leave Dev without telling him why or when she would return, and it hurt her so much. But with her gone Esther and Dev would be safe. She hoped Abdul and his men captured the rebels soon, so King Ahmed would be safe as well.

Felicity felt a loyalty to Dahrain if only because of Haaji. She'd met Ahmed a few times, but she had been struck by his fine intellect and his deep devotion to his people. The small part she could play in somehow protecting the democratic leader of Dahrain would be her memorial to the wonderful man who had protected her for so long.

She opened the doors of the huge closet that took up one entire wall of her bedroom and tried to focus on choosing a dress for dinner. Con, Heller, and Pacer were coming and she wanted to look her best. She was eager to become a friend to the beautiful woman Con had married.

No matter how hard she tried she couldn't seem to keep her mind on anything as she got ready for dinner. She slipped on a turquoise silk dress and lightly applied makeup. Her freshly washed hair was flyaway, and she twisted it into a French braid that hugged the back of her head.

Her shaking hands put on one emerald earring and one topaz. "Stop that," she muttered. "Settle down or Dev will see right through you."

She stared at her reflection in the mirror on the dressing table, taking deep breaths. She was too pale, she thought. Her cheekbones looked chiseled, harsh, her neck too long and slender to hold her head. Mentally shaking herself, she tried to put steel into her spine.

Stepping into two-inch heels, she sighed. She would still be many inches shorter than Dev. Dev! How could she leave him even for a few days?

She glared at her mirror image. "Stop it!"

Changing her mind about her jewelry for the tenth time, she stared down into the open box on the table. Haaji had been most generous with her, and she smiled as she looked at the assortment of precious gems.

Not all her urging him to be sensible had stopped him from buying her expensive baubles. In fact, it had seemed to give him more joy than it had given her.

Deciding on the oval-shaped sapphire earrings as her only adornment, she sighed again. Tomorrow she would be leaving Dev, and it hurt so much more than she would have imagined. . . .

"I knocked but you didn't hear me."

She swung around. "No, I didn't hear you." She eyed Dev in his dark evening suit. How could she have forgotten how devastatingly handsome he was? Now that he was older he had developed a patina of sophistication, but it barely masked the rawness of the man underneath. Dev had always been a gentle savage.

"Your hair has blue lights in it from the sapphires and your eyes are brighter than the jewels."

Breathless, she laughed. "You could have given Byron lessons in poetry."

He ambled across the room to her. "You're too beautiful. You always have been."

Their mouths touched briefly.

"I didn't know it was possible to be too beautiful."

"Only you have managed it."

She reeled at the throbbing in his voice. He was making love to her with words. She was naked and vulnerable to him and it stunned her. The tongue that had often probed her in lovemaking was now weaving cobwebby passion around her being. "Are the Wendels here yet?"

"Why is your voice so hoarse?"

She cleared her throat. "It's not."

He touched an earring. "Did he give them to you?"

"Haaji? Yes, he did."

"They're beautiful."

"Yes." She braced herself for the arrogant demand that she not wear them.

"I will never ask you not to wear them, Felicity."

"Obviously you've changed in some ways." She caught her breath at the violence that flashed across his face like a summer storm, then was gone. "Do we know each other at all?" she whispered.

"Probably not, but even in the closest of relationships people change and have to adapt. *C'est la vie.*"

He moved closer, his mouth touching hers once more. Lifting her left hand, he studied it for a moment. "You removed his ring."

"Yes."

"Will you wear this one?" He pushed a pear-shaped sapphire onto her finger, kissed the stone, then looked up at her. "It's the color of your eyes."

"It's . . . magnificent. I've never seen anything like it."

"Con, Pacer, and I went to Princeton with a man who now owns an exclusive jewelry store in New York. If you notice Heller's ring, a rare wonder, it was purchased from the same man."

When Felicity would have removed the ring his hand covered hers. "Wear it please."

"Dev, I'm not sure this is a good—"

"Let's just take it one step at a time."

He hauled her against his chest. "I need you with me."

"Dev," she murmured, her arms circling his back, her eyes closing. It was so wonderful being with him, loving him, having him. . . .

"Should I go out and come in again?"

"Dammit, Pacer, you pick your times." Dev kept his arm around Felicity as he turned to his friend.

Pacer leaned indolently against the doorjamb. "Are you going to greet your other guests?"

"Yes, damn you, we are." Dev's growled response drew a chuckle from Felicity and Pacer.

Con and Heller were in the enormous living room. When Felicity and the two men entered, Heller squeezed her husband's hand.

"Yes, sweetheart," Con said, "I see." He chuckled softly. "Dev looks like a lighted Christmas tree. Only Felicity was ever able to do that to him."

"Shh."

Pacer had heard the exchange as he crossed the room to them. "Darlin', you're just never going to get used to the way we discuss one another . . . in front of one another."

Heller smiled. "Probably not."

Felicity walked over to them and kissed Con, then hugged Heller. "I never got used to their ways either. Have you been thrown off balance by the way one starts a sentence and another one finishes it?"

Heller nodded. "Having all three of them in one room at the same time is almost frightening." She leaned down and whispered in Felicity's ear, "You brought him back from the dead, you know."

"Thank you. I guess I've come back to life too."

Con walked over to Dev. "How did we get so lucky?" he asked, nodding to the two women.

Dev shook his head. "Beats me, but I'm not questioning anything."

"I've a good mind to move in on both of you," Pacer drawled. "I'm sure those discerning ladies would prefer the better man."

"Not if he was dead," Con said lightly.

"Or maimed," Dev added.

"There is that." Pacer grinned, then ambled over to the bar in the corner. "I'd like a beer, and the two women would like seltzer and lime, if I recall correctly."

"We could just break his legs," Dev said musingly.

"True." Con leaned against the mantel and gazed at Dev. "Things are better, I assume."

"Yes. Felicity seems content here. At last."

Pacer paused in the act of taking the two drinks

to the women. "Remember there's still danger here. We don't know who the enemy is yet, old chum."

"Pacer's right," Con said. "I have a feeling we'll know more soon, but for now . . ."

"The danger is very real," Dev finished. "I know that, but at least she's here, under guard."

Pacer nodded and continued on to the women, who were seated on the sofa and chatting animatedly.

Con eyed his friend. "I haven't seen you this relaxed in years, but there's still something eating at you, isn't there?"

Dev shrugged. "I guess I won't feel a hundred percent relaxed until we've taken care of the threat to her and Esther."

"We'll do it." Con lifted his glass and toasted his friend.

Pacer returned in time to see the gesture, and lifted his beer as well.

Dev smiled at his friends. "Thanks."

"No thanks needed," Pacer said. "You know that." He glanced at Heller and Felicity. "They are the best and deserve every care."

"Amen," Con murmured.

Dev nodded, his gaze touching Felicity and staying there.

Seven

Felicity waved good-bye to Esther as the limousine pulled away, taking her daughter to spend the day with the Wendel twins. Dev had already left for Manhattan. He had decided he didn't want any outsiders at his mountain hideaway, even associates he trusted. Their earlier good-bye had been passionate. Almost too passionate.

"Umm," Dev had murmured, "if that's a sample of what I can expect when I return, I'll be hurrying all day." He kissed her again, his lips lingering, his tongue pressing against hers. "You excite me, darling."

"You light a pretty good fire yourself," she said, trying to catch her breath.

She ran her fingers over his face. Fooling herself into thinking she had put him out of her brain had not made it happen. Too much of her belonged to Dev.

Taking her hand, he kissed her fingertips. "What are you thinking?"

"How easily you've taken over my life again."

"I think the reverse is true, lady."

"Do you, now?"

He nodded, staring at the sapphire ring he'd given her. "I want to marry you again, to take away any problems of legality we could run into. When will you let me put a gold band behind this one?"

"Dev," she crooned, kissing his ebony hair as he bent over her hand. "Give it time."

"Too much time has been wasted, Felicity. I lost you and Esther." He held her close, letting his mouth rove her face. "Put me out of my misery and marry me, Felicity."

She grasped his head and looked up at him. "We still need more time, Dev. We're so different now. I was independent when I married you, and when I married Haaji I was even more independent. Though I didn't officially have a job, I was his counselor and closest adviser. There was nothing in his life he didn't tell me." She released Dev and stepped back. "Your features haven't changed, but I can tell you're surprised. Most people would be. Though Haaji was a Dahrainian, he was also very liberal. He not only believed in the rights of women, he thought that many of the world's female leaders had done better jobs and been more progressive than the men."

"I would say he was an unusual Dahrainian," Dev drawled.

She tapped his nose with one finger. "See! There is a great deal of anger and unresolved feelings between us."

"It doesn't mean they can't or won't be settled. Other married couples do it all the time. And so will we." He kissed her. "See you tonight and keep this thought." Clutching her to him, he pressed his mouth to hers, his tongue intruding, touching. "I need your fire, Felicity," he told her hoarsely. Then he released her, spun on his heel and went out the door.

She could no longer see Esther, and Felicity felt teary and ineffectual. Even if only briefly, she was leaving the two people she loved most in all the world. How was she to deal with that? Why not chuck it all and let Dev handle it. No! He would never back down. The terrorists would soon know that and target him.

Pushing aside her blue thoughts, she stepped back into the house and ran up the stairs to her room. Packing very few clothes in order to look inconspicuous, she took only what fit in her canvas carryall. She would return to Dev. She would.

The autumn day was chilly, so she threw a suede jacket on over her blouse and soft corduroy slacks. The moment of truth was at hand. Between them, she and Abdul would bring about a peaceful solution and she would come home again.

It was Dutch comfort, but all she had.

Taking a deep breath, she descended the back staircase of the sprawling stone mountain home, hoping she wouldn't run into the housekeeper.

The fewer people who saw her leave the less information could be forwarded to Dev. Besides, she didn't want to talk to anyone. If she did, she might cry. Of course, there was always the chance she wouldn't be able to sneak away in a car. Dev had insisted she have a chauffeur at all times.

She shivered as she pictured Dev's reaction. He had been a bulldog reporter. Once he had an idea or suspicion in his mind, nothing got in the way of his resolving it, one way or another.

Crossing the empty kitchen, she inhaled deeply to calm herself. The quick beat of her heart didn't slow. She stepped out the back door without having seen anyone. Getting to the spacious garage attached to the stable would be another matter. She was halfway there when a man appeared beside her.

"Good morning, Mrs. dai Haaji. Would you like me to drive you somewhere?"

Felicity schooled her surprise into a semblance of a smile. "Oh, there's no need, Rendoll. I can drive myself. I'm just going into Woodbourne for a few things."

"No trouble, ma'am," the burly man said, his easy tone not disguising his determination. "Mr. Abrams wants you to have an escort wherever you go, ma'am."

"Ah . . . fine." Abdul had better be in that back alley. There would be just so much stalling she would be able to do. "Shall we go?"

The drive along the corkscrew road into the small town was beautiful, with the autumnal colors at their height. Russet, gold, green, and red vied with the glorious blue sky for attention as the car swept smoothly around the hairpin curves of the mountain road leading into Woodbourne.

Rendoll stopped in the small public parking lot and prepared to accompany her.

"No need for you to come," Felicity said, smiling winningly. "I'll be right over there." She pointed to the general store on the north side of the main street.

"All right. I'll walk over with you and wait outside."

No way was any employee of Dev Abrams not going to be thorough, she thought, swallowing a sigh. "I might be a while. I want to look through all the fabrics they have in there."

Rendoll smiled slightly and nodded. "No trouble, ma'am. You just take your time."

The crossed the street and Felicity entered the store. Glancing out the large front window, she could see Rendoll had stationed himself right beside the door.

Taking deep breaths to calm herself, she looked around the store, relieved there were other customers. She noted the aisles of goods were higher than her head. Bolts of cloth were stacked precariously along the narrow walkways. Was there a rear entrance? Had to be. Would the back door be open? Up one aisle, down the other. A fresh breeze wafted across her face. She turned eagerly toward it.

If anyone stopped her she could say she was looking for the ladies' room. One more glance over her shoulder at Rendoll, then she was moving swiftly into the back area. Here again she encountered merchandise piled so high, the place was like a maze. Moisture beaded on her lip as she looked around and opted for the aisle to her left. Dead end! Back tracking, she prayed she would remain unseen. She turned down another aisle, then another, then . . .

The back door was in front of her, and it was ajar. She pushed it open wider and stepped out into the alley. Before she had a chance for more than a cursory glance around, Abdul was there, his hand on her arm.

"Wow. That was efficient," she said. She tried to smile, but now that she was here, all she wanted to do was run back to Dev and throw herself in his arms.

"This way, madame. We brought a van, so that you could be totally concealed in the back."

"Good."

Abdul hustled her to a brown van. The man behind the wheel of the running vehicle was a stranger to her. Opening the back, Abdul helped her inside, then hopped in beside her.

"You stay back here, madame. You'll find that bench seat quite comfortable. I'll ride up front with Hatan."

She nodded. She was barely seated when the van roared down the alley and careened onto the main street. "Abdul," she called as she righted herself on the seat. "Aren't you afraid you'll get stopped, driving that way?"

A few guttural Dahrainian words steadied the

driver. Felicity glanced up front and was startled when she saw the driver was watching her in the rearview mirror, his dark eyes opaque and expressionless. She had to fight shudders that rose in waves through her body.

"So you stopped to pick up your daughter yourself," Heller said to Dev, kissing him. "She's a beautiful child and so intelligent. But I can see by her absorption in every game the children play that most of them are new to her. I think your daughter hasn't had much time to be a child."

He nodded. "That doesn't surprise me. It's a very cruel world in the Middle East. Children's needs are not a high priority. Most youngsters her age are already learning to be soldiers."

Heller's expression became solemn. "Have you found out anything about the people who could be after Felicity?"

"Not much. I'm tempted to call Dahrain and speak to the king about it."

She chuckled. "Trust you to think of that."

"I'm serious."

"I know. What does Felicity say?"

"She doesn't know. When I called the house just before lunch to tell her I'd be back early, she'd gone out with Rendoll. I'll talk to her at home. How do you like your stay in the mountains?"

"I love it." She smiled. "Neither Con nor I could remain in the city knowing you need support."

"And I thank you for that. Come on, beautiful lady, show me my child."

When they reached the game room, they paused in the doorway, watching the children's antics as they played charades. Esther was spellbinding as she pirouetted and swayed to music only she could hear.

"Prima ballerina?" Heller whispered.

"Who knows? I'll ask her if she'd like lessons with the New York City Corps de Ballet."

"Starting at the bottom, are you?" Heller smothered a laugh when Dev grinned.

"My daughter deserves the best."

"Well, she has a good start with such great parents."

"Thank you." He kissed the top of Heller's head.

"It's a good thing I'm not the jealous type," Con drawled at their backs.

Dev turned. "But you are, Con. Everyone knows that."

He shrugged. "Heller's my weakness. We all have one."

"True." Dev smiled when his friend gave his wife a passionate kiss. "Branding her?"

"I've been trying, but I think I'm one who's been marked for life."

"You'd better believe it," Heller said, more than a little flushed by her husband's embrace. She leaned against him and looked toward the room. "We were just remarking on Esther's grace as she acts out her charade."

"She's a lovely child. Has Dev signed her with the Bolshoi yet?"

Heller's laughter turned the heads of the children.

"Is it time to go home now?" Esther asked Dev.

"Yes, sweetheart. But maybe you can come back tomorrow. Would you like that?"

"Yes." She shyly slipped her hand into his and smiled up at him. Dev felt his heart soar once again.

"I'd better get going—"

"Pardon me, madame," the Wendels' butler interrupted. "There's a call for Mr. Abrams."

Dev took the portable phone from the man. "Abrams. What? When? Have you searched the area? Do it again. I'll be right there." He shut off the phone, fighting the nausea that threatened to overcome him. "They have her," he told Con and Heller quietly.

"Damn." Con tightened his hold on his wife. "Heller . . ."

"I'll keep the children here," she said quickly. "Find her, Dev."

"I will." His words were a vow. He lifted Esther into his arms and kissed her. "We've decided you can stay here with your cousins for a while longer, sweetie. I'll see you soon."

As though his tension had touched her, she clutched her neck. "I want to go with you." Her voice was reedy and uncertain.

"Not to worry, precious. I'll be back for you." He kissed her cheek. "Daddy loves you."

She looked at him solemnly, then hugged him. "Come for me soon."

"I will." He passed her into Heller's arms. Then,

with one last look at his daughter, he sprinted from the room.

"What the hell happened?" Con asked, keeping pace with his friend as he leaped down the stairs. "I'll call for the chopper."

Dev waited impatiently as Con made the call, then the two men left the house on the run.

"Rendoll thinks Felicity slipped out the back door of a store in town," Dev said as they ran for the Jeep.

"Are you saying she handed herself over to them?" Con aimed the Jeep across the grass, forgoing the paved road that led to the pad.

"It looks that way. My wife has a misguided sense of duty, it would seem." Dev grated the words.

The pilot greeted both men with a smile that died at Con's first command.

"Get it up there fast."

"Yes, sir, Mr. Wendel."

Neither man spoke during the short journey. Dev was sure his brain would explode if he tried to talk. Every energy cell in his body was concentrated on Felicity. What in hell had she done? Why had she done it?

The helicopter landed at Dev's, and both men leaped out as it barely touched ground.

Pacer was waiting behind the wheel of a Jeep. Con and Dev jumped in and Pacer sent the Jeep hopping over the ground like a scalded cat.

"Nothing new, Dev," he said, "but I do have some people working on this already."

"You warned them to be careful."

"These guys might be mercenaries, Dev, but they know who you are, and what would happen to them if Felicity wasn't returned in perfect health."

"We'll find her, Dev," Con said quietly.

"We have to." There was a death knell sound to Dev's voice.

At his house, Dev raced inside without waiting for Con and Pacer. The two men glanced at each other.

"He's on fire," Pacer said.

"A human torch."

"Con, he'll kill the first person he sees who's had anything to do with this."

"I know. When his blood is at the boil like this, there's no stopping him."

"When you'd been captured that time in 'Nam, he turned into a killing machine. He didn't even hear the major say there was no way to get you out." Pacer paused. "I damn near couldn't catch him then. I don't know if the two of us will be able to handle him now."

"Maybe we'd better just stick with him, no matter what."

Felicity was tired. It seemed as though she'd been in the back of the van forever. "Abdul? Are you taking me to the consulate?"

"Not exactly, madame."

"Where, then?"

"I will take care of everything, madame. We will reach our destination soon."

"Good. I'm getting very tired of this van."

"I am sorry for the inconvenience, madame."

"Do you know any more about the people who may be plotting to kill the king?"

"Yes, madame. We are fairly sure we know who the men are."

"Really?" She straightened. "Even the ones who killed Haaji?"

"Yes, madame."

"Abdul, that's wonderful. Then I'll be able to return home soon."

"I'm sure things will work out satisfactorily, madame."

She covered her mouth to smother a yawn. "Did anyone ever tell you that you're the soul of discretion, Abdul?"

"No, madame, no one has told me that."

Nor did he have a sense of humor, she thought tiredly.

After another hour, when Felicity was dozing, the van came to a stop and the back door was opened. She blinked against the sudden light. Her watch read eleven o'clock. It was a cool, crisp day, but the sun was shining brightly. She leaned forward and took Abdul's hand as he helped her to the street.

"Where are we?" Looking around, she frowned. "Why, this is the apartment building. Why are we here?"

To get something, madame. Come, you should not be on the street."

She nodded and followed him through the glass doors. The van driver was right behind her.

Won't you get a ticket leaving the van parked out front?" she asked Abdul as they stepped into the elevator.

"The van has been taken away."

She turned to face him. "Why are we here, Abdul?"

The blow caught her on the side of the head, blacking out the world.

"There was no need to hit her so hard, Hatan. We do not want her dead."

"Now we have her. Soon we'll have the king."

"Quiet. It's not time to gloat yet."

"Soon the country will be ours and the old ways of our people will rule." Hatan nudged Felicity's inert body with the toe of his boot. "Women like this should be destroyed."

"Haaji believed she was touched by Allah." Abdul felt a sudden chill and looked around.

"Bah. Allah would have nothing to do with such a woman."

"Who's he calling?" Pacer asked Con as he strode into the study. He had just been questioning Rendoll again. "Rendoll says she took a tote bag with her, but she could have put some clothes into it easily."

Con nodded. "I'm not sure, but I think Dev's called the king of Dahrain."

Pacer whistled softly. "Isn't that just like him?"

"I've never seen him quite this bad."

Pacer stared at Dev. "Carved from ice."

"I told you," Dev said into the phone, his voice tight and impatient, "I want to speak to him because it's to his benefit and mine. It's about the death of his uncle, Haaji dai Haaji."

Dev glanced up at Con and Pacer. "Damn, I'd be quicker flying my own jet to Dahrain and—yes? Your Highness, my name is Deveril Abrams and I'm . . . I see. Jarred Hamilton has already told you who I am." Dev frowned and the other two men moved closer to his desk, Pacer perching on one corner, Con slouching into a chair. "Yes, sir, I have every intention of remaining a husband to Felicity. Sir, I would love to chat with you at any other time, but there's something urgent that I need to tell you." Dev tersely explained to the king what had happened, then said, "Do you mind if I put you on a speakerphone, Your Highness? I have two friends here who are helping me find my wife. Thank you, sir." Dev pressed a button and the king's voice came over the wire.

"Who do you think has taken Farisa . . . ah, Felicity?"

"I was hoping you could help there, sir. We are assuming Felicity contacted someone who helped her get away from here. I think she believed my daughter and I would be in danger if she stayed. There was already one attempt on her life."

"I see. I do not know why the rebels who are

causing such unrest in my country would want to kill Farisa. But I will ask my people here to see what they can find out. I will do what I can to ensure the safety of Felicity. My people honor her as I do."

"Your Highness, my name is Pacer Dillon. Are you sure there isn't any reason why the rebels would kidnap Felicity at this time?"

There was a short silence, and the three men exchanged glances.

"No, not really," the king said finally. "I will be in New York on Monday, but I don't see any connection there. No, I don't know a reason why she should be taken at all."

"Thank you, Your Highness."

"Ah, Mr. Dillon, I will tell you that my uncle set up most of the security for my trips and his methods are still used. Sometimes he had elaborate plans." The king's voice faded. "I don't suppose that would mean anything now. My uncle has been dead for some time."

"Who will coordinate your security in New York, sir?" Dev asked brusquely.

"Abdul ben Hashallah, my uncle's trusted lieutenant."

"I met him the first night I saw Felicity," Dev murmured to Con. "Intelligent, tough."

Con reached for another phone. Pacer loped out of the room.

"Thank you, Your Highness," Dev said.

"Mr. Abrams, I hear pain in your voice. I will

talk to my people here immediately. Between us, we should be able to free the beautiful Felicity."

"Your Highness, did Haaji or any of his people ever intimate that it would be dangerous for you to come to this country?" Dev's harsh question was followed by a sudden silence.

"Mr. Abrams, how is it that you know this?"

"An educated guess. Am I on the mark?"

"Yes. Shortly before my uncle was killed, he told me he was worried about penetration of the security system. He didn't know who the enemy was, but he felt he was close. At that time I canceled a trip I was to make to your country. For the good of my people I must go to New York this time. There will be no cancellations," the king said firmly.

Con put down the phone he was using and reentered the conversation. "My name is Con Wendel, sir, and I have an army of security people whom I can place at your disposal."

"Many thanks to you, but all is in order for this trip."

"Very well, sir. It would help if we coordinated our searches for Felicity, if possible. How could we contact your security people here?"

"Call the consulate. I will get you clearance."

"Thank you, Your Highness. We will keep in touch." Dev added his thanks, then hung up.

"I think the king might have a skunk in the woodpile," Pacer said, sitting again on the edge of the rosewood desk.

"Do you think Haaji was assassinated because he knew who it was?" Con asked.

"It's a place to start," Dev said frostily.

"You're getting a prickly feeling about this, aren't you?"

"Yes," Dev said. "The first night I met Felicity she was with two men. One was Abdul, the new head of the king's security. The other was a lawyer, Jarred Hamilton, the man who told the king about me."

"I know Hamilton," Con said. He got Hamilton's office number from Directory Assistance, then barreled his way through a receptionist and a secretary to get to the man. "It's Con Wendel. I was wondering if you could tell me anything about King Ahmed's visit to this country on Monday. Yes, I know it's confidential . . ."

Pacer turned to Dev, who was staring out the window, his hands flexing and unflexing. "She'll be fine, Dev."

Dev didn't turn around, the stiff set of his shoulders telegraphing his pain. "She has to be."

When Con got off the phone he was frowning. "Hamilton says there hasn't been even a whiff of trouble and he's talked to the consulate several times in the last few days."

"Would they confide in him?"

"I don't know, Pace. Maybe." Con looked disgruntled.

Dev wheeled around and strode to the phone. "Dahrainian consulate? I need to contact a member of the staff. Abdul ben Hashallah. Thank you, I'll wait." He covered the mouthpiece with his hand. "Maybe he can help us— Yes, I'm here. I see. Could

I give you my number so that he could call me? Thank you." Dev hung up and shook his head. "That's odd."

"What?" Pacer asked.

"They wouldn't give me an address or a phone number, but they'd take a message. Since he's out of town, they couldn't promise he would get back to me right away."

"You would think he would be in town if the king is coming here in three days," Con said musingly.

"And maybe we're reaching," Pacer said.

"Maybe." Dev looked thoughtful. "Felicity's apartment in Manhattan might be a good place to start looking."

"Why don't I call Karim before we do anything?" Pacer asked.

"Karim Adal? From Princeton?" Con nodded. "He's Dahrainian, isn't he? Go ahead, Pacer, do it."

"Isn't he royalty in Dahrain?" Dev asked.

Pacer nodded as he reached for the phone.

"I'd forgotten that connection," Con said, steepling his hands in front of him.

"I shouldn't have. He's been in the papers often enough since he became Dahrainian ambassador to this country." Dev smiled. "I had dinner with him a couple of years ago. He's not the freewheeling gagster he once was, I will tell you that."

"None of us is, friend."

"True."

• • •

Dev poked at the food in front of him, then reached for his coffee and swallowed some of the scalding brew. "Why the hell doesn't anyone call?"

"Because there's nothing to report," Pacer said laconically. He speared the steak on Dev's plate and lifted it onto his own. "Relax. It's in gear and it's moving."

Dev rested his chin on his hand. "Do you think she's all right?"

"Yes." Con rose from the table. "I'm going to call Heller."

Pacer watched Con leave the room. "I do believe he can't breathe for long without that woman."

"Believe it."

"And you are every bit as bad with Felicity."

"Yes," Dev said hoarsely.

The phone rang. Pacer answered it, spoke briefly, wrote something on a pad of paper, then hung up.

"Well?" Dev asked.

Pacer took Dev's baked potato too. "You know what you were saying about Abdul being out of the city?"

Dev immediately went still. He had learned long ago to listen to Pacer when he had that pensive tone. "Yes."

"Karim thought it strange too. Abdul apparently was supposed to be in New York this week. Karim tried to contact him and got the same story you did. He thought Abdul had been called back to Dahrain, sort of undercover. He called Dahrain and was told Abdul was in New York." Pacer glanced at what he'd written. "This is the address."

Dev took the paper. "This is the address of the apartment building where Felicity stayed."

"I smell a rat."

Dev jumped to his feet. "I'm going into Manhattan."

"You smell one too?"

"Yes."

"I'm with you."

"No! You stay here. I want you to call your contact in the CIA. See if there's any connection between Abdul and these terrorists. The barest thing will do."

"Family, politics, and all that jazz," Pacer drawled. He dabbed at his mouth with his linen napkin. "Con won't like you bugging off like this."

"I'll keep in touch. I'm taking the chopper."

"Right. Dev, be careful. It won't do Felicity much good if you get killed."

"I've thought of that."

"Good. We'll be right on your tail."

"I know."

"Watch her," Abdul growled. "One of you remain outside this bedroom at all times. The door to the sitting room will be locked, as will the hall door to the bathroom."

"Why are you doing this, Abdul?" Felicity asked. "Haaji trusted you."

"It is not for you to speak about men's business. If you were a proper woman, you would say nothing."

"Be a slave, you mean, like so many of the hill women."

Abdul's eyes flashed. "Women have not the souls to understand the work and words of men. Therefore they should be quiet." He pointed his finger at her. "Now you will be silent and say no more." He looked at his men again and spoke in a rapid Dahrainian dialect. Felicity understood enough to know she would be killed if she tried to escape.

He glanced back at her. "You will remain in this room and not try to enter any other."

She could barely quell the shiver that coursed through her. Abdul must have been hand in glove with the assassins who'd killed Haaji. Had he set it up?

"This evening might be your last alive, madame." His smile was evil. "Then again, we may save you for a special occasion. On Monday the king will be here. He will be expecting to see you. How discourteous if we did not allow that to happen. Wouldn't it be fitting if you and he should die together, the king and the wife of Haaji the traitor. Then the world will see what we do to all traitors."

He stared at her for a long time, and Felicity didn't even swallow. It was not the time to bait or prod Abdul. The deck was stacked in his favor.

Then he was gone, his men at his heels.

Finally she was alone. Tremor after tremor shook her frame. She would never see Dev and Esther again. But they were safe. Abdul had not said he would harm them. What good would it do him anyhow to go after Dev, perhaps create an international incident that could backfire? But would that stop Abdul if he made up his mind to harm Dev or Esther? She hadn't missed the fierce, fanatical look in his eyes.

Why hadn't she seen Abdul's perfidy before? Why hadn't Haaji? How long had he been working with Dahrainian dissidents who wanted to overthrow the government? She felt stupid and inept. Had Haaji been killed because he suspected Abdul? Her mind whirled like a dervish as she tried to make sense of the mess.

Abject grief caught in her throat. She had just found her beloved Dev again. They'd been together such a short time, and now she had to lose him once more.

Woolly-headed, she stared around the room she'd stayed in so briefly a few weeks ago. Or was it a million years ago?

She was immobile for a long time, her brain like oatmeal, refusing to accept the reality of what was happening. Then, as though the perils of the situation stung her to life, anger began to simmer in her. This was her country; she was in New York City. How dare foreigners try to intimidate her! If she was going to be killed anyway, there was no reason to hold back. She would go down making as much trouble for Abdul and his people as she could.

Haaji had always stayed in this apartment when

he traveled to the United States. After they were married, he asked her never to go abroad with him, believing an assassin would have better luck killing him outside of Dahrain. Although she'd never accompanied him, he had told her about the alarm network he'd had installed in the apartment. Remember, remember.

His room! He had mentioned a system of alarms in his bedroom that would alert the police and fire department. They were hidden in a stereo speaker.

Make noise. Create diversions. More than once Haaji had told her to gather as many people around her as possible if she felt threatened. Force the adversary to concentrate on more than his target.

Getting off the bed slowly, she took deep breaths. There was a shivery feeling on her skin as though the men guarding her out in the hall could see what she was doing. Perhaps that wasn't so strange. How simple to have a monitor in the room to observe what she did. Haaji had never mentioned a monitor, but he had been a cagey man. Best to operate on the theory that she was being watched.

Abdul watched Felicity on the small television screen. He hoped she would show him a hiding place somewhere in the room. Haaji had never trusted anyone completely, and there were several secret agents in Dahrain whose names Haaji had never revealed to Abdul. He needed to know who those men were and kill them. Nothing would be permitted to halt the coming revolution.

The phone rang, and he frowned. "Yes? Oh, it's you. Stop whining. I am sure this Mr. Wendel is no cause for concern. What do you care? You have been well paid for your services. No, I will not change my mind." Scowling, Abdul slammed down the phone. He turned to one of his men. "I think Mr. Jarred Hamilton might betray us, Omar. See to it that he cannot."

Omar bowed and quickly left the room.

Abdul turned back to the television. He needed that list of agents! He had ordered men to search Haaji's home and office, but they had found nothing. This apartment was the only other place Haaji had spent much time in. Damn him for the canny devil he'd been. At times Abdul had to remind himself that the greatest enemy to the cause had been dead for a long time, because there were moments when Haaji seemed to hover over him.

At least Haaji had been a fool about the woman. Perhaps she would reveal a secret place. If she didn't, he would try torture. Madame Haaji dai Haaji's life was of no importance.

It would give Abdul great satisfaction to see Haaji's woman dead. Too long he had pretended it didn't bother him to converse with a woman as though she were his equal. Vinegar in his throat would have been sweeter. Now she would die as Haaji died. Soon the old ways would come back to his country.

"Keep your eyes on her," he ordered his other

guard. "If she opens up a safe or a hiding place, mark it well and call me. At once."

Knowing Haaji, Felicity was sure there were several avenues of escape from the apartment. With that in mind, she moved around the bedroom, idly touching things. Let someone watch her! Much good it would do.

Her brain clicked over every bit of information she could dredge up, all the conversations she'd had with Haaji that might apply. Her eyes flashed around the room, though her movements were slow.

She wandered back to the right side of the bed. Haaji always slept on that side, no matter where he was. He also always kept a gun beside him, sometimes taped to the inside of the bed board. Would there be one in this room?

There had to be something, anything that could give her an edge.

She spotted the speaker first, almost abutting the bed at mattress level. Did Abdul know about it? Probably. He'd been so close to Haaji. But . . . Haaji had been fanatically careful. Various individuals would have information about Haaji, but no one person would know every detail of his security.

Taking a deep breath, she sat down on the bed and pulled onto her lap a magazine that had been on the bedside table. She leaned back against the headboard, and let her right hand drift down as her left hand languidly turned the pages. Where would a camera be? Overhead? On the wall?

Lazily, she pulled the comforter from the foot of the bed over her, screening her movements somewhat.

Turn the magazine pages. Her right hand had fixed on the speaker. Fingers probing over the surface, she searched for something. . . . She felt the front of the speaker move sideways.

Without looking, she pressed every button she felt, again and again. Hopefully she'd set off an alarm somewhere. Then she pushed the speaker cover back in place.

Still moving slowly, she let the magazine slide off her lap. She got off the bed to pick it up, and searched the side of the bed for a weapon. Nothing. Wait! After much groping, she felt cold metal.

God! She was perspiring so much.

An Uzi! She could tell by the shape. Haaji's guards had carried them. The handgun that had the versatility and power of a machine gun and the accuracy of a pistol was a lethal weapon.

She yanked it free and hid it under the magazine, then lay down on the bed again, the gun a comforting weight on her lap.

Had whoever was watching her seen the weapon?

How would she know if it was loaded? She wouldn't. It was a chance she would have to take. At least she had a better shot at freedom than she'd had a few minutes ago.

• • •

Abdul's guard stared at the screen. The woman was nervous. It was as though she felt his gaze. He had no intention of telling the quick-tempered Abdul such a thing, though. Getting struck by the butt of a gun as Hamid had yesterday was not something he relished. And Abdul had been quick to do that when Hamid had displeased him.

Besides, she was merely a woman and not worth watching. What could she do?

Dev landed his helicopter on the roof of a building owned by Con. Security was a little annoyed with him. Precious time was used up explaining his presence, but his call to Con relieved the suspicions of the guards.

"Look, call the police and tell them where I am," he instructed them as he left. He gave them the address of the Dahrainian apartment building.

He took a cab and had the driver let him off a block from the building. Counting on his knowledge of expensive housing in Manhattan, he circled the building to where its underground garage opened onto the street.

As he walked down the ramp, he decided to alert the security guard. He stayed in the shadows as he approached the kiosk, a safety maneuver held over from Vietnam. He could see before he was seen. There was a man in the kiosk. Dev stood motionless, studying the man for a moment. Silent alarms went off in his brain when the guard moved into the light.

He was young, dark, and muscular. He had the look of young men Dev had seen every day when he'd been in Beirut and Iran. Maybe it was a coincidence. There were many dark-skinned, dark-haired men in New York. Dev Abrams was one of them.

The sixth sense that had been his friend in Vietnam, his companion in many dangerous situations, was tingling now. He watched for several minutes. When the guard turned to pick up the phone, his back was to Dev. Dev took the opportunity and moved deeper into the garage.

He was at an impasse. He couldn't go up in the elevator unless he had a key. Staying in the shadows for what seemed like hours, he was rewarded when a car drove down into the depths and parked.

Moving easily as though he'd just come from a car, too, he followed the man toward the elevator and stepped into it just behind him. "Saves me from getting my key out," he said genially to the man who barely glanced at him.

The man punched one floor, Dev another.

Dev got out on the floor below the penthouse apartment. He carefully opened the door to the stairs, checking for guards. No doubt they were at the bottom of the stairway, discreetly out of the way so as not to alert the suspicion of the house security.

Dev climbed upward, to the roof.

Saying a prayer that there was an outlet from the penthouse to the roof, he opened the door at the top of the stairwell. Before him was an empty hallway, lit only by one lamp. The air was tinged with the smell of chlorine.

The door facing him was unlocked. Opening it a crack, he saw the pool. The area was dark. He could barely discern the Plexiglas roof that protected the pool. Was Felicity really here? Or was this a wild-goose chase?

Taking deep breaths to calm himself, he slipped inside the room. How was it that whoever was holding Felicity didn't know about the pool door? Did that mean she wasn't in this building? No! Don't start thinking that way, he told himself. This was the best shot. He would find her and get her out.

He let his eyes adjust to the dark, then moved slowly toward the glass wall that separated the pool area from another hallway. If his sense of direction was accurate, that hallway should lead to the penthouse.

Trying the door to the hallway afforded him a jolt. It was locked. He removed a long thin burglar's pick from his wallet and probed the lock. If he set off an alarm, he could be caught before he had a chance to look for Felicity. Dammit! He couldn't let that happen.

Click! It sounded so loud. Opening the door a fraction, he waited for alarms. After a few quiet moments he slipped into the hall, moving slowly, crouched and ready.

When he heard voices, he moved past a room fast. Standing in a shadowed corner, he counted to ten before continuing on. He was about to round a corner when he noted a mirror up high near the ceiling. If he moved, his reflection would be visible to any guard who cared to check.

Looking around, he spotted another door. Locked. Again he used the pick. Sweat beaded his brow. Someone could come out of any of the doors behind and in front of him. Hurry!

The door opened into a dark room. He slipped inside, then shut and relocked the door. Not far from him was another door. Enough light seeped in from under it to let him see he was in a bathroom.

He crossed the room silently and put his ear to the door, but heard nothing. He took a deep breath, let it out slowly, and turned the handle of the door, opening it a crack.

Felicity was sitting on a bed looking his way. A magazine lay across her lap. Under the pages was an Uzi pointed right at him.

He was about to open the door wider and step into the room when he caught the almost infinitesimal shake of her head. She rolled her eyes toward the ceiling.

Was there a monitor there, he wondered, an electronic baby-sitter? Was it even now watching him in the bathroom?

Signaling to her, he waved her his way.

She slipped off the bed, magazine in hand, the gun still hidden. Moving unhurriedly, she walked into the bathroom and closed the door behind her.

Dev caught her in his arms and kissed her long

and hard. Then he put his mouth to her ear. "Win, lose, or draw, we're in this together."

Felicity nodded, feeling the dampness on her cheek. His hell-for-leather grin had her heart thudding against her ribs. The danger was real and immediate, but Dev was beside her. She could reach out and touch the man who filled her life. She wasn't afraid.

"We'll only have a few minutes," he said softly. "Let's go."

She shoved the Uzi into his hands. "I recall you were pretty good with a gun."

He hefted it and nodded. Then he opened the hall door.

Felicity stayed right behind him, touching his back. When he pressed her hand in encouragement, she closed her fingers around his for a moment.

The hallway was still deserted, but Dev could hear a shuffling from around the corner. It was the guards, he assumed, who were stationed in front of Felicity's room.

He led her away from them, back toward the pool area. Determination rode him like a bull. He'd either get her out, or he'd die in the attempt.

Her fingers touched him gently, telling him she was right on his heels.

He wanted to turn and sweep her into his arms, but he pushed the thougt from his mind and concentrated on their escape. The stairway leading from the pool was their best bet, but once the alarm was sounded, that area would be swarming with guards. It would be too much to hope that Felicity still had her elevator key, or that she had it with her. No time to ask her.

The man monitoring the television screen looked up at it again, frowning. The woman still hadn't returned from the bathroom. American women primped. Unlike the women in the mountains where he was from, American females painted their faces, fussing over themselves. They masked what beauty they might have. Fools!

But . . . what if she was trying to get out the bathroom door? What if she had some way of working the lock? Bathrooms might have nail files. He knew what they were. His years in the United States had taught him much.

His hand hovered over the alarm button that could be heard throughout the apartment. No! Better to check with the other guards.

He glanced at the monitor again, then left the small room. He didn't want to be right, or wrong. Either way could go against him. Allah curse the foreigner. Guarding the woman was a nuisance. Why didn't they just kill her?

They were in the hall that led to the pool area when Dev heard the sirens, signaling the approach of emergency vehicles. Since it was not an uncommon sound in Manhattan, he was sure the guards would take no notice. Too bad. The diversion would have helped.

"I set off some alarm buttons in the bedroom," Felicity whispered. "I hope that's the answer."

Damn! What a woman. "With a little luck it could be." He smiled at her and kept moving, praying the distraction would be the edge they needed.

At last they reached the door to the pool and he pulled Felicity through behind him. Never had steamy, chlorinated air been so welcome.

"That is quite far enough." The man's voice cut through the misty air like a knife through soft butter. "We want the woman."

Dev saw the man as he lifted his gun. It *was* Abdul. Abdul fired, and the shot almost grazed Dev's left cheek.

He threw Felicity behind one of the lounge chairs, knowing it was a damned poor shield against automatic fire. Crouching down near her, he aimed his gun and fired.

The pool door burst open and two Arab men ran in. Dev shot at them and Dahrainian curses filled the room. A pain-filled scream echoed off the walls, then there was return fire.

Noise burst the eardrums! It was every Fourth of July rolled into one. Bits of tile rained down like tiny missiles.

Felicity tried to see, but she was afraid to do much more than turn her head slightly. She couldn't really help Dev, but perhaps she could make sure no one approached them from the back.

The moist atmosphere picked up the powder from the ammunition, creating a dense fog that made seeing almost impossible. Dev blessed the fog even as he cursed their chances. One man did not have the spread of several automatic firearms.

When she saw Dev's body jerk, Felicity knew he'd been hit. Without thinking she crawled to him as fast as she could.

"Just a graze, darling," he said. "Stay down. We're not beaten yet."

"Are you sure you're not seriously hurt?"

He nodded, his smile twisted. "I've gotten worse falling into the gutter. It's time to change our position. We'll get behind that waist-high tile divider. Stay on your stomach and crawl toward it. Don't stop until you get there." He pushed her. "Go!"

Felicity did as she was told, praying that Dev was right behind her. When she heard Abdul's voice above the din, she faltered.

"Madame, listen to me! Come out now and you will have a chance. If you do not, you will be killed and we will go after your daughter. Do you understand?"

Dev pressed his hand on her back. "Keep moving, darling."

She heard the anger in his voice. She nodded and crawled the last few feet, panting as she turned to look behind her. Dev was there.

He put his mouth to her ear. "They just want to pinpoint us. If you've set off alarms, people will be answering them. Our safest bet is to stay low and hold them off. Pacer and Con will be here soon."

All at once the lights went on in the pool, banishing the semidarkness that had protected them.

The gunfire increased to a crashing level, shaving off even more knifelike shards of tile. Dev knew it was only a matter of time before they were spotted. Then the firepower would be concentrated.

"Listen to me. Go out the door behind you and down the stairs. That's the way I got in."

She stared at him and shook her head. "No, I won't leave you."

"Darling, please, think of Esther. I love you." His urgent whisper was loud in the sudden stillness, then the shooting began again. "Go!"

"Esther needs both of us."

He knew Felicity meant what she said. He fired at a shadow that flitted closer than the others. The man's yell attested to the accuracy of his aim. "We'll both try it. Go first."

Felicity wriggled on her belly to the door, reached up, and turned the knob, then she was out of there.

Crouched down, Dev backed toward the door.

"Stay still." Abdul was beside him, his gun pointing down at him. "Put your gun on the floor. Don't try anything."

Dev laid the gun down and straightened.

"Where is the woman?"

"I don't know."

Abdul struck Dev across the face with the gun.

Dev sank to the floor, barely aware of more shouting across the pool.

The best chance of escape was diversion, he thought fuzzily, fighting to stay conscious.

"Kill the woman!" Abdul shouted angrily. "Kill them all!"

Dev realized several men had forced their way into the pool area and were fighting with the Dahrainians. Maybe it was Con and Pacer, maybe the authorities. Whoever it was was coming on strong. He had to make his play now. If only the blood weren't running in his eyes.

Dev's face throbbed. He had to stay awake, alert. The odds were better now. He could save Felicity, and maybe himself. She was already on her way down the stairs. Covering her escape was paramount.

When Abdul stepped over him, apparently heading for the stairs, Dev reached for him and missed. The man was moving fast. He was going after Felicity!

Shaking his head to clear it, he staggered to his feet, trying to keep the man in sight. Had the vermin guessed that Felicity had gone down the stairs? If so, Dev had to follow him. No one was getting to Felicity.

It wasn't until he was out the door that he remembered his gun. No time to go back for it now.

He swiped at the blood that blinded him, then took a deep breath and listened. There was the echoing sound of footsteps racing down the stairs.

Were there two sets? His fuzzy brain gave him no answers.

Steadying himself, he hurried down the steps, not even trying to mask the noise he was making. Speed was more important than silence.

He looked over the railing down the open stairway. A bullet whined past his ear. Abdul was both angry and alert, and he was still following Felicity.

Pulling back, he took a deep breath and shouted as loud as he could. "Run, darling, and keep going. Pacer or Con will be on the street." He took the steps two at a time, hugging the wall as he tried to close with the man who could kill the woman he loved more than life.

Once he tripped and fell sprawling, the wound in his side burning as though someone had put a match to it. His face thudded as if a thousand hammers were playing on it. Felicity!

Again he looked over the railing. He'd gained on Abdul. Hurrying now, he calculated where he could make the most effective move. The steps seemed to whirl in front of his eyes as he raced down them.

Another glance showed him Felicity far below and Abdul dangerously close to her. Dev leaped down to the next landing, but realized with a doomsday certainty that he wouldn't be able to stop Abdul before he could catch Felicity or shoot her. He had to do something. Fear was acid in his mouth.

With fearsome determination, he leaned over the railing and called to Abdul in insulting Farsi.

When the man turned to fire upward, Dev backed away. Abdul looked back down and Dev vaulted the railing, throwing himself, feetfirst, down the stairwell.

If he missed, he would continue downward for more than ten stories. His momentum might pull the man with him, not stop his hurtling body.

He saw Abdul turn, saw him bring up his gun. The movement was too late. Dev slammed into him, the force of his body jamming him against the railing and almost sending him over. Dev crashed against the railing as well, breath whooshing from his lungs.

For long moments the two men were draped over the railing, Dev's lower body swinging free as he grappled with Abdul. His fingers digging into the man's face, Dev knocked Abdul's head against a steel stanchion. He wasn't sure, but he thought he heard the other man's skull crack.

Hanging on to Abdul, his legs wrapped around the stanchion, he tried to pull himself up.

"Need some help?" Pacer was there, lifting him over the railing as though he were a sack of meal and depositing him on the stairway. "Con's coming. He'll take care of things."

Pacer glanced at the man sprawled unconscious on the stairs. "You put him out for the count, chum."

"Good," Dev said, panting.

"That was some jump. I thought you were gone for sure." Pacer smiled, but the hand he reached down to his friend was shaking. His eyes stung, as the fear of what he'd seen Dev do rolled over him once more. "You were always damned impulsive."

"Yeah," Dev muttered. "Let me go. I have to see Felicity."

"Okay, I'll carry you." Pacer hoisted Dev into his arms, noticing how he flinched. "Take a bullet?"

"Creased in the side. Had worse."

"I remember. Your face looks terrible and you have a knot on your head. Felicity'll probably choose me now."

"The hell you say," Dev mumbled, his head on Pacer's shoulder.

Pacer pulled open the steel door on the landing. "I don't suppose you mind if we take the elevator down, do you? You're no lightweight."

"Don't mind," Dev answered, smiling weakly, his eyes closed.

Pacer got him into the elevator and continued to hold him. Dev's face had a grayish tinge, and Pacer had to swallow the fear that rose in his throat. How bad was the wound? Dev was a master of understatement.

In Vietnam he and Dev had rescued Con, and Dev had covered their retreat single-handedly while he helped Con. Pacer shook his head. Confident, determined, and unafraid Dev. He'd taken a bullet then too . . . and more.

Pacer recalled how cockily Dev had called to them to climb aboard a truck, then driven like a bat out of hell, gunfire all around them. Not until they were safe did Pacer discover one of Dev's legs had been torn up by shrapnel and he'd been hit in the side. "Damn you for being reckless, Dev," he muttered.

When the elevator doors opened onto the lobby, Con was there, gun in hand. He sucked in an angry breath when he saw Dev being carried by Pacer. "Damn, Heller will have my eyes if he's hurt badly."

"Just a crease, the man says." Pacer looked down at his now-unconscious friend. "Damned near gave me heart failure, Con. He jumped over the railing and down the stairwell to get the guy following Felicity. If he'd missed, he would have gone clear to the bottom."

"My God." Con touched Dev's face as emergency medical aides laid him on a stretcher. "Felicity's outside. I'd better get her."

"Hell! He'd better be okay." Pacer gave his friend a lopsided smile. "He just came to life after he'd been dead for so long, Con. Can't lose him now."

"We won't. Damn him for the chances he takes." Con turned to walk alongside Dev, then rushed ahead when he saw Felicity being restrained by two policemen. "It's all right. Let her through."

"Con, is he . . . ?"

"He's unconscious, but he's tough as old boots. You know that, Felicity."

She nodded as the stretcher was rolled out. Then, leaning over Dev, she said, "Dev, don't leave me." Anguish laced her voice.

Dev's face twitched as though through the fog of unconsciousness he heard her.

The three clambered into the ambulance, crowding the attendant, who glared at them.

"Pacer," Felicity said, "I saw him jump over the railing . . . I think. It was such an insane thing, I can't believe . . ." She shook her head. "Did I see right, Pacer?"

He nodded, his face tight. "I've seen him do some wild things, but . . . damn, I can't describe that piece of lunacy. How the hell he calculated that, I'll never know."

Felicity's gaze moved to Con. "He'll be all right, won't he?"

Con swallowed, then nodded, but his gaze slid to the attendant, who looked concerned.

There were no more words as the three friends watched Dev and the man who worked on him.

At the hospital, they wouldn't be separated from him, so they watched the emergency team through a glass window.

"What happened to Abdul?" Felicity asked, her gaze fixed on her man.

"If he's the one Dev collared, he's in intensive care," Pacer said shortly.

"He planned it all, even Haaji's death," Felicity explained. "King Ahmed is coming to New York Monday and must be informed of this." She inhaled shakily. "Abdul had planned to kill me along with the king as a show of strength to Dahrainians."

"Dev wouldn't have liked that," Pacer said woodenly, staring at the operating team.

"The Dahrainians must know what happened," Felicity said.

"I'll take care of it," Con whispered, glancing at Pacer. Time enough to tell her about the death of Jarred Hamilton and his probable part in the conspiracy."

"He has to live, you know," Felicity said. "It can't happen again. Too cruel." Her voice cracked.

"It won't." Pacer put his arm around her.

"I love him so much, Pacer. Life without him was so—so mechanical."

"Shh."

"When I was with Haaji, I was fine because I could live for Esther and be of some use, but I'd put my feelings away, you see. Then Dev came again and brought me back to life."

"It will be all right, Felicity." Pacer kissed her hair.

"I'd still have to live for Esther, but I will be dead without Dev . . . I won't like that."

The matter-of-fact way she spoke alarmed Conrad. "I'll get some coffee."

Pacer kept his arm around her, murmuring words of encouragement. When she looked up at him, her gentle smile broke his heart. She was so vulnerable, so exposed to pain. "We'll pull him through, Felicity."

"We must."

"And we will."

Eight

Dev opened his eyes and smiled lazily at Felicity. "Stop looking at me as though I'm breakable, darling. I'm just fine."

"Maybe so, but the doctor says that you suffered a severe concussion along with the bullet wound and you need rest and care." The nightmare of Dev jumping down the stairwell was with her yet.

"Don't, darling. I know you're thinking of that time in the stairwell."

She swallowed and nodded once, reaching out to touch him. "It's—it's a good thing I'm tough."

"Beautiful and tough," he murmured, kissing her hand.

"You're a daredevil."

He smiled. "Actually, I'm a pussycat."

"I want you back to full health. You lost a great deal of blood."

"That was weeks ago, love." He gazed at her,

wondering if he would ever be able to banish totally the fear he sometimes saw in her eyes. "Shall we go for a walk, maybe take a swim later?"

"If you like." At times Felicity felt she would never get enough of looking at him. Almost losing him for the second time had caused unbearable pain.

"Let's go," he said.

"I like Barbados; it's paradise. And Con and Heller's place is lovely." Felicity had been happy at the big white house that faced the Caribbean. She'd needed the time alone with Dev, if for nothing else than to satisfy herself that he was really all right.

"And Esther likes being with her cousins." Dev smiled as he thought of his child. "She's so beautiful, just like you."

"I can tell she has come to love you, Dev."

He nodded happily.

It was late afternoon, nearly dusk. The sudden wonderful setting of the sun was like the boom of a cannon. One moment it was full daylight, then a flash of sun, sometimes with a streak of emerald green along with the mauve, coral, and purple, then it was full night. The sunset never failed to enthrall Felicity. It was over in a blink of an eye, but so splendid in that instant. Only a tropical sunset had such wonder.

She and Dev would watch the magic kaleidoscope from their terrace or as they strolled the beach, but always they would be holding hands, touching each other.

Felicity had to be joined to him. She needed the

connection of flesh as much as she needed food. Hadn't she almost lost him again? That near loss had wounded her soul.

Dev, being Dev, had strained himself too much after his wound, lost too much of his precious blood. What should have been a relatively simple operation to remove a bullet became a battle to save him when he'd gone into shock. It had been all the horrors of her life rolled into one! It was still with her at times.

People touched her, talked to her, but her being had shut down. At times she didn't hear even what Pacer, Con, or Heller said to her. All her concentration had been on Dev, as though by sheer force of will she could make him live.

When he'd finally turned the corner and begun to get well, she'd almost collapsed from the loss of energy, from tying herself spiritually to him, concentrating totally on him.

Slowly, agonizingly, Dev had fought, coming back by inches, then by leaps and bounds, his wife always with him.

Esther had been tearfully delighted to see her father home again, though she'd been shocked at his weakness. She had clung to him and told him she'd make him cookies, and that he could ride her pony anytime he wished.

He had hugged her as though she'd just been returned to him. He hadn't hidden his feelings. Tears had moistened his cheeks as well.

"Why are you smiling, darling?" Dev put his arm around her. He had to touch her all the time.

It still seemed ridiculous that they were together, that she was his again.

"I was thinking of Esther promising to make you cookies every day of your life if you would get well."

Dev stopped walking, his smile rakish and happy in the fading light. "That's right. I'm going to call her tonight and demand that she get started. Let's see. How many days of backlog is that? I want my full share." He grinned at Felicity. "She's wonderful, just like you."

"Me? No way; she's like you."

Dev preened. "Yeah? I like that. Heller said she had my spirit."

"Not that, please. I don't ever want her taking the chances you do." Felicity shuddered, her mind cartwheeling painful images behind her eyes.

Dev knew by her expression she was recalling her escape from Abdul. He could kick himself for triggering that memory for her. "Now, honey, you know that's behind us and—"

"And you jumped down a stairwell like some kind of—of madman!" Her eyes widened as she turned to face him. "I can't forget what you risked for me."

"Don't be a dope," he told her huskily. "In saving you I was saving myself, just being selfish." He leaned down and kissed her nose. "I need you."

She curled her arms around his neck. "I couldn't have lost you again. Not possible."

The sheen of tears in her eyes jarred him. She'd been so vulnerable, so shaky since her kidnapping.

"Darling, don't. Abdul has been taken back to his country to be tried for his crimes. He won't get off easily, I don't think." Dev looked grim. "It wasn't all bad. I don't think King Ahmed will ever be so gullible about those around him again."

"Or about Americans he believed were his friends." She shook her head. "I never thought Jarred Hamilton would betray his friendship with the king and Haaji. He was Haaji's friend."

"If it's any consolation, I think he was backing out of the deal and that's why Abdul had him killed."

She nodded sadly. "King Ahmed was completely serious when he said he wanted you and Pacer to set up a security system for him."

Dev's smile was crooked. "And he kept asking me how to take out the enemy quickly."

"That was after Pacer described what you'd done. Ahmed is no slouch himself when it comes to action, so he admires you very much."

Dev shook his head. "His kingdom is a time bomb. The Middle East is a tough world."

"Yes, but I'm glad the three of you are going to give Ahmed a hand. He is a fine young man, and truly cares about his people."

They went quite a distance along the beach, until Dev noticed the beading of perspiration on her upper lip. "Ready for a swim?"

"Very."

They strolled back toward the beach house, hand in hand.

Felicity could feel his gaze on her. "What is it?"

"I don't know. There's some new dimension to you, but I don't know what it is."

She laughed, and the sound rippled over him like the sweetest caress. His hand tightened on hers. "I like it best when you do that when we make love."

"Sounds like a good idea."

He closed his eyes for a moment. "But you'll want to swim first and I won't be decent in my suit because I'll be thinking about what we're going to do when we get out of the water. You should be ashamed of yourself, Mrs. Abrams."

She leaned on him. "I like the sound of that. Mrs. Abrams." Suddenly she straightened. "Are we married, Dev? I mean, I was married to Haaji . . ."

"We're married. I checked it out."

She stopped and touched his cheek. "Is it too hard for you to live with? My marriage to Haaji, I mean?"

"No, it isn't. I just try to smother the thought of you married to anyone but me." He held up his hand when she would have spoken. "It isn't just the sexual thing, love. It's knowing that you shared those precious intimate moments that loving married people have. I want those all to myself."

"And now you have them."

He grinned crookedly. "Yes."

She strolled ahead of him into the spacious

home, heading straight for the bedroom, occasionally slanting glances at him.

"Are you keeping something from me, Wife? You have that look about you."

"Now, would I do that?" She grabbed her little nothing of a suit and went into the bathroom.

In moment she was out again. Dev had already pulled on his suit, and her gaze riveted to the red scar at his waist. She swallowed the painful panic that seeing that mark brought and sidled past him, her fingers trailing over his chin.

"You look sexy as hell in that string bikini," he muttered. "I hope no one comes along our beach. Damn, what a lovely view." He followed her through the sliding doors from the bedroom to the terrace. "Felicity, I think you've filled out since we've been together." He was proud of that. "You needed the weight."

"Not nice to remind a woman she's put on weight."

He took her hand as they crossed the white sand and entered the water, their overheated bodies shocked by the sudden coolness, though the water was actually warm and delightful.

In lazy strokes they swam out toward a wreck about a half a mile out. On the trip back, Felicity stayed close to Dev, her hand occasionally feathering over him. When she touched his lower body, she grinned at the instant reaction.

"Damn you, woman," he said lovingly.

"How you talk! I only wanted to tell you something, so I had to get your attention." She laughed when he turned on his back and pulled her to him.

"You have my attention, as always."

She kissed him, wanting him, loving him. "We're going to have another baby, Dev. It's pretty early, but I can tell."

Dev sank like a stone, then surfaced, sputtering. "Are you sure? Is it all right? Can we?"

She saw through his little-boy smile to the lacing of fear behind it, and threw her arms around him, taking them both to the depths of the blue-green sea.

When they surfaced, Felicity knew it wasn't just seawater running off their faces. "We're fools, aren't we, Dev, for not knowing we had the answer to life."

"Yes. Let me help you back. I don't want you to tire."

"Not much chance of that when I'm all fired up to make love."

He laughed, swallowed water, and coughed. "Damn, how could I forget how sexy you were when you were carrying Esther?"

"I know." She turned on her back and let him tow her, though she was perfectly capable of swimming in herself. "You'd be working on a column and I'd look at you and feel as though steam was coming out of my ears."

Dev's feet hit bottom. He was about to swing her up in his arms when she stood, too, and held her hand out to him.

"Oh, no, you don't. Carrying me is still down the road for you, Deveril Macklin Abrams."

He would have argued with her, but her chin was out and he knew that she wasn't going to bend on this one. "All right, this time. But I reserve the right to change those plans in a few days, lady."

"Make it a few weeks and you'll get no quarrel from me."

Arms around each other, they strolled to the house, entering from the terrace to the bedroom.

"What are you thinking?" she asked, noticing his pensive expression.

"Have you seen a doctor?"

"Not yet, but I will when we get back to New York. I thought Heller would be a good one to consult about that. Why are you laughing?"

"Because you'll have thirty doctors then. Con was a mess when Heller was pregnant. She'd been through so much and it scared him that she might not be up to delivering a child." Dev smiled down at Felicity. "But she's like you, tough and beautiful."

"Thank you." She still noticed a certain concern in his look. "But my pregnancy bothers you, doesn't it?"

"To be honest, yes. You had a hard labor with Esther."

"But very fast."

"Speedy, that's you." He reached for her. "I need you, Felicity. I have since that night in London when you kicked me in the shin."

She pressed her lips to his neck and chuckled. "I

remember. How did I ever dare do such a thing to the great Dev Abrams?"

"God, your lips feel wonderful against my skin."

"Sensuous devil." Hesitantly, she looked at him, and he led her to the bed.

Dev felt as though the world were spinning off its axis. His libido was climbing into overdrive as he strove to keep himself on keel. "I love you, Felicity."

"I know, and I feel the same."

Raging desire telescoped into tender passion as each tried to pleasure the other. Sweet memories joined with a sultrier present as their lives melded into one joyful pocket of time.

Dev and Felicity were one again. Love had carried them through the maelstrom and joined them. Dev was the blue flame, the hottest fire, consuming the pain, giving them joy, and joining him and Felicity for all time.

THE EDITOR'S CORNER

With the very special holiday for romance lovers on the horizon, we're giving you a bouquet of half a dozen long-stemmed LOVESWEPTs next month. And we hope you'll think each of these "roses" is a perfect one of its kind.

We start with the romance of a pure white rose, **IT TAKES A THIEF**, LOVESWEPT #312, by Kay Hooper. As dreamily romantic as the old South in antebellum days, yet with all the panache of a modern-day romantic adventure film, Kay's love story is a delight . . . and yet another in her series that we've informally dubbed "Hagen Strikes Again!" Hero Dane Prescott is as enigmatic as he is handsome. A professional gambler, he would be perfectly at home on a riverboat plying the Mississippi a hundred years ago. But he is very much a man of today. And he has a vital secret . . . one he has shouldered for over a decade. Heroine Jennifer Chantry is a woman with a cause—to regain her family home, Belle Retour, lost by her father in a poker game. When these two meet, even the sultry southern air sizzles. You'll get reacquainted, too, in this story with some of the characters you've met before who revolve around that paunchy devil, Hagen—and you'll learn an intriguing thing or two about him. This fabulous story will also be published in hardcover, so be sure to ask your bookseller to reserve a collector's copy for you.

With the haunting sweetness and excitement of a blush-pink rose, **MS. FORTUNE'S MAN**, LOVESWEPT #313, by Barbara Boswell sweeps you into an emotion-packed universe. Nicole Fortune bounds into world-famous photographer Drake Austin's office and demands money for the support of his child. Drake is a rich and virile heartbreaker who is immediately stopped in his tracks by the breathtaking beauty and warmth of Nicole. The baby isn't his—and soon Nicole knows it—but he's not about to let the girl of his dreams get out of sight. That means he has

(continued)

to get involved with Nicole's eccentric family. Then the fun and the passion really begin. We think you'll find this romance a true charmer.

As dramatic as the symbol of passion, the red-red rose, **WILD HONEY,** LOVESWEPT #314, by Suzanne Forster will leave you breathless. Marc Renaud, a talented, dark, brooding film director, proves utterly irresistible to Sasha McCleod. And she proves equally irresistible to Marc, who knows he shouldn't let himself touch her. But they cannot deny what's between them, and, together, they create a fire storm of passion. Marc harbors a secret anguish; Sasha senses it, and it sears her soul, for she knows it prevents them from fully realizing their love for each other. With this romance of fierce, primitive, yet often tender emotion, we welcome Suzanne as a LOVESWEPT author and look forward to many more of her thrilling stories.

Vivid pink is the color of the rose Tami Hoag gives us in **MISMATCH,** LOVESWEPT #315. When volatile Bronwynn Prescott Pierson leaves her disloyal groom at the altar, she heads straight for Vermont and the dilapidated Victorian house that had meant a loving home to her in her childhood. The neighbor who finds her in distress just happens to be the most devastatingly handsome hunk of the decade, Wade Grayson. He's determined to protect her; she's determined to free him from his preoccupation with working night and day. Together they are enchanting . . . then her "ex" shows up, followed by a pack of news hounds, and all heck breaks loose. As always, Tami gives us a whimsical, memorable romance full of humor and stormy passion.

Sparkling like a dew-covered yellow rose, **DIAMOND IN THE ROUGH,** LOVESWEPT #316, is full of the romantic comedy typical of Doris Parmett's stories. When Detective Dan Murdoch pushes his way into Millie Gordon's car and claims she's crashed his stakeout, she knows she's in trouble with the law . . . or, rather, the

(continued)

lawman! Dan's just too virile, too attractive for his own good. When she's finally ready to admit that it's love she feels, Dan gets last-minute cold feet. Yet Millie insists he's a true hero and writes a book about him to prove it. In a surprising and thrilling climax, the lady gets her man . . . and you won't soon forget how she does it.

As delicate and exquisite as the quaint Talisman rose is Joan Elliott Pickart's contribution to your Valentine's Day reading pleasure. **RIDDLES AND RHYMES**, LOVE-SWEPT #317, gives us the return of wonderful Finn O'Casey and gives him a love story fit for his daring family. Finn discovers Liberty Shaw in the stacks of his favorite old bookstore . . . and he loses his heart in an instant. She is his potent fantasy come to life, and he can't believe his luck in finding her in one of his special haunts. But he is shocked to learn that the outrageous and loveable older woman who owned the bookstore has died, that Liberty is her niece, and that there is a mystery that puts his new lady in danger. In midsummer nights of sheer ecstasy Liberty and Finn find love . . . and danger. A rich and funny and exciting love story from Joan.

Have a wonderful holiday with your LOVESWEPT bouquet.

And do remember to drop us a line. We always enjoy hearing from you.

With every good wish,

Carolyn Nichols

Carolyn Nichols
Editor
LOVESWEPT
Bantam Books
666 Fifth Avenue
New York, NY 10103